KU-433-922

Friedrich Hölderlin, one of the greatest poets of the Romantic Period, was born in Germany in 1770. He enrolled as a student at Tübingen Seminary in 1788, but by the time his studies were completed he was at odds with official religion and already absorbed by the classical themes and pantheistic philosophy that were to shape much of his future work. To support himself he turned to tutoring, and it was while serving in this capacity in the household of a Frankfurt banker, Gontard, that he fell in love with his employer's wife, Suzette, the "Diotima" of *Hyperion*. In 1798 this relationship caused his abrupt dismissal from his post. He completed his novel, *Hyperion,* and continued to write poetry whose lyricism and philosophic harmony place it in the first rank of German literature. But by 1802 he was no longer sane. He was placed first in an asylum, then boarded in the home of a Tübingen carpenter, where he remained in a state of harmless delusion. Translations of Hölderlin's poetry into several languages have brought about his recognition as one of the great poets of Western civilization. Outside of Germany, his novel *Hyperion* is less well known. It is now presented in an English translation for the first time.

HYPERION

or

The Hermit in Greece

Friedrich Hölderlin

Translated by Willard R. Trask

With a Foreword by
Alexander Gode-von Aesch

A SIGNET CLASSIC

Published by The New American Library,
New York and Toronto
The New English Library Limited, London

CAREFULLY SELECTED, EDITED, AND PRINTED,
SIGNET CLASSICS PROVIDE A TREASURY OF THE WORLD'S GREAT
WRITINGS IN HANDSOMELY DESIGNED VOLUMES.

Copyright © 1959, 1965 by Willard R. Trask
Foreword Copyright © 1965 by
The New English Library Limited, London
OF WORLD LITERATURE, INC.

First Printing, September, 1965

SIGNET TRADEMARK REG. U.S. PAT. OFF. AND FOREIGN COUNTRIES
REGISTERED TRADEMARK—MARCA REGISTRADA
HECHO EN CHICAGO, U.S.A.

SIGNET CLASSICS are published *in the United States* by
The New American Library, Inc.,
1301 Avenue of the Americas, New York, New York 10019,
in Canada by The New American Library of Canada Limited,
295 King Street East, Toronto 2, Ontario,
in the United Kingdom by The New English Library Limited,
Barnard's Inn, Holborn, London, E.C. 1, England

PRINTED IN THE UNITED STATES OF AMERICA

HYPERION

or
The Hermit in Greece

FOREWORD

I

HÖLDERLIN'S *Hyperion* is not difficult in itself. Great works, almost by definition, seldom are. But it is easy and in a sense natural for us to fail to see and hear what is there when we come with fixed preconceptions of what should be there.

Hyperion was written as a novel, and has been and will be read as one. But it is more than a formal paradox to say that to read this work as a novel in the conventional sense is to misread it. Perhaps we should make more of the fact that it is a *German* novel, at the risk of getting involved in some rather inextricable contradictions.

There is indeed something a bit "aside" about the history of the novel in German letters. Its ultimate origins in the medieval epic do not differentiate it from the novel in other national literatures, and its climactic accomplishments in the twentieth century (with names like Thomas Mann and Hermann Hesse) again put it in the mainstream of a universally occidental continuity. But what and where is it between? In particular, what can be said about the German novel in the eighteenth and nineteenth centuries, i.e., during the period that encompasses all the great names of the English, the French, the Scandinavian, and the Russian novel?

If we start our quest for the German novel with criteria taught us by Dostoevski or Dumas or Dickens, we do not, to be sure, find altogether nothing, but what we do find cannot, somehow, fully measure up.

Two disparate observations need to be made at this point, and both have a crucial bearing on Hölderlin's *Hyperion*. One is that in the great narrative tradition of occidental literature the more succinct novelistic subform of the novella has been a more characteristically German preoccupation than the more comprehensive and perhaps more rambling novel. It is not always easy to maintain a clear definitional separation of the novel and the novella, but the presence of a single, simple, more or less neatly statable thematic problem will always tend to make us classify a particular work as a novella rather than as a novel. In this sense the (to many) greatest German "novel," Goethe's *Elective Affinities,* is not perhaps a novel at all but a novella. And so is Goethe's *The Sorrows of Young Werther*. And so is, quite definitely, Hölderlin's *Hyperion*.

The second observation concerns the semantic range of the German word for "poetry," i.e., of *Dichtung*. It is not adequately rendered by "poetry," for the verb *dichten* still carries the meaning of its Germanic forebear, "to dress, dispose, order, shape," though a subsequent association with the Latin *dictare* restricted the range of the term to the creation of order, and hence of beauty, of words. While it is only by extension that English permits us to speak on occasion of a novelist as a poet, the German term *Dichter* refers naturally to any creative writer, regardless of whether it is his individual lines that are subject to laws of form, of rhythm and rhyme, or whether the total conception is meant to reflect the inner form of an organic microcosm.

Hyperion—like *Werther,* like Novalis' *Ofterdingen,* like many another German novel or novella—is a *Gedicht,* and *Gedicht*—as applied to *Hyperion*—is a word we need not hesitate to translate into English as "poem."

This is more than a taxonomic nicety. It implies a demand for a fairly radical shift in the reader's criteria, for the grandeur of a poem lies rarely in the closed perfection of the finished product; it lies more generally in the intimation of what the work would be if the poet were really a god. Thus seen, the greatness of a poem is of necessity the greatness of failure. The poet is a tragic figure in that he cannot but attempt the impossible, with longing or aspiration as the surrogate of attainment.

II

Hyperion has been called a Greek *Werther*. This is a neat formula, but if it does suggest some significant affinities, its foremost merit is that it makes us more keenly aware of the characteristic differences between the two works.

Goethe's *Werther* appeared in 1774, the two parts of Hölderlin's *Hyperion* in 1797 and 1799. During the intervening quarter century the explosive success of *Werther* engendered a string of imitations of ebbing appeal, and insofar as *Hyperion* does belong in this continuity, it is not hard to understand that it evoked a comparatively weak echo.

Werther was a young man for whom the problems of puberty and epistemology, i.e., of love and religion, were too much. He stands, historically, where the coolly confident rationalism of the eighteenth century abdicates in favor of the ebullient stress and storm of the romantics and, biographically, where Goethe achieved adulthood.

The artistic form that Goethe chose for his *Werther*—regardless of literary models and precedents—was the

only one possible and adequate: that of a novel in letters.
It is a one-sided correspondence. The addressee of the
Werther letters, Wilhelm, never replies and remains pale
and fictitious. If he were objectively real, his intervention
would arrest the subjective outpourings that are the essence
of *Werther*. He is not even allowed to take over when
Werther is dead. The concluding report is contributed by
an "Editor," who is uninvolved and therefore exempt from
the risk of being resented by the reader as an intruder.

Hyperion is likewise constructed as a sequence of letters.
The addressee, Bellarmin, is the same throughout the entire work, and like Werther's friend, he never replies.
The one exception to the rule of uniformity in *Hyperion*
is that Hyperion entrusts to his friend, as an enclosure to
one of his communications, a packet of letters he has exchanged with Diotima before her death. But this does not
disrupt; it actually strengthens the impression that the entire work emanates from a single subjective "I."

If we add to this the fact that the unobtrusiveness of
the editor of Werther's letters is further emphasized in
Hyperion—there is no editor at all, for Hyperion does
not die within the confines of the novel—we can hardly
find it surprising that *Hyperion* continues to be misclassed
as a Greek *Werther,* i.e., as a record of the subjective emotional outpourings of a soul in distress.

Actually, the rhapsodic style of *Hyperion* is the vehicle
of much highly unemotional thought, of considerable learn-
ing, and even of delightfully homespun truths. Hölderlin's details of Greek geography and his descriptions of
the Greek landscape (which he had never seen) are exact
and based on the study of sources that scholars have been
able to trace with chapter-and-page precision.

However, the structural characteristic of *Hyperion* that
puts it poles apart from *Werther* is that the Hyperion
letters are not diarylike descriptions of synchronous experiences but retrospective reports. It is a passionately
lived life that the "hermit" Hyperion recalls and describes,
but he describes it without passion, as something that was
and is no more, like a dream of error and effort, devoid

of spontaneous pain and joy, and without real bearing on either the present or the future.

The first two letters of the complete series of forty-five that make up the two parts of *Hyperion* are the only ones written throughout in the present tense. In these, Hyperion reports to Bellarmin (whom he met during his sojourn in Germany) that he has returned home to Greek soil, living now the quiet and detached life of a "hermit," wondering how he could ever have thought that life and action and endeavor might lead somewhere.

At the beginning of the third letter Hyperion thanks Bellarmin for having asked him to recount his life, of which the remaining forty-two and a half letters represent then a progressive confession and apologia.

There can be no tense and worried uncertainty as to how "it will all come out" on the part of either Hyperion himself or even the reader. As Hyperion describes to Bellarmin his early childhood—primarily the impact left on him by his transient teacher Adamas (who had come from afar and went on afar on an ineffable quest)—he writes of course in full awareness of all the subsequent events and alludes to them frequently. As one reads on one senses that Hölderlin consciously guards against the emergence in his readers of sympathizing fears and emotional hopes. When Hyperion meets the glorious figure of Alabanda, who looks like a young god descended from Olympus, we know—half by intuition and half by Hölderlin's hints —that this is the expected guide into the arena of fore-doomed material endeavor. When after the abortive uprising of the Greeks in 1770, from which Alabanda expected glory and achievement for both Hyperion and himself, the young god from Olympus must die, we are sad but not shocked. We foresaw nothing else.

Quite early in the sequence of Hyperion's letters to Bellarmin there appear allusions to Diotima. And when Hyperion describes his first meeting with her, he knows (and we know) that she is already dead. In a way one might say: There are no occurrences in *Hyperion;* there are only facts, immutable facts of existence; Diotima is dead.

III

Hölderlin was the most Greek among the German Greeks, and there were many of them.

Much has been written and said about the German *Drang nach Osten,* and rightly so. The German "pressure eastward" in European political history corresponds remarkably to the American "pressure" to the West, and failure to heed this would cripple our comprehension of the sequence of past, present, and future.

There was also—and still is—the German *Drang nach Süden,* harder to describe and harder to account for without trailing off into mystical speculation, but more essential to the German cultural, literary, and spiritual endeavor.

The statement that the German language is the most Latin of all modern languages is an objective (though not generally recognized) fact. Beyond this, however, there is the more essential, less tangible, and more nostalgic German-Greek linguistic affinity. It constitutes a particularly characteristic problem in the appreciation of Hölderlin as an artist. We need but allude to the frequently made observation that Hölderlin's language in its maturity—in the great odes, "Patmos" and "Bread and Wine," and above all in *Hyperion*—was German only in its verbal raw material but Greek in essence and spirit.

The names that come to mind as one tries to suggest the major phases of the German-Greek affinities are Winckelmann, Goethe, Hölderlin, Nietzsche. None of these four ever set foot on Greek soil. Winckelmann was murdered in 1786 by a purse-snatcher near Trieste and never had a chance to experience Greek realities more directly than through their colonial reflections in Italy. Goethe, in his wisdom, stipulated Greece to be the reality he needed to substantiate a vision and did not query beyond "sending the soul to seek the land of Greece," as he had his Iphigenia put it. In Hölderlin the tragic fear appears that perhaps the "real" Greece does not and cannot exist.

There is in Hölderlin's "Greekness" something remarkably new, something of which there is no trace in the earlier German-Greek tradition, something that may account for his modernness, for the appeal he has for us today.

It is by no means that Hölderlin marked a break with the romantic idolization of Greece, that he replaced the idealized concepts of Winckelmann or even Goethe by a keener, more critical, and shrewder appraisal of Greek realities. He took no such step. That remained for men of a later generation.

The Greek nostalgia of Hölderlin, in its supreme manifestation in *Hyperion,* is unique. The fact that the hero, Hyperion, is Greek—modern, eighteenth-century Greek— is more than a random detail. Consciously considered by the poet or not, to the reader it has symbolic significance. The Greek ideal, romantically longed for, appears poignantly not beyond but within. Romanticism, as it were, has lost its distance. And equally significant though less apparent on casual reading, when this Greek, this Hyperion, does translate the goal of his quest to geographical distance, he travels to Germany. He goes there in a vaguely desultory way. It does not seem to matter very much. And the degeneracy of the Germans that he notes does not come as a shock to him. Why should they differ from his countrymen?

What sounds like didactic preaching in *Hyperion* appears always concerned with a subsequent phase of additional dimensions. "It was no man that you wanted," says Diotima to Hyperion, "believe me, you wanted a world." And the work as a whole stands under the motto: *Non coerceri maximo, contineri minimo, divinum est* ("Not to be confined by the greatest, yet to be contained within the smallest, is divine").

The two quotations match. The individual life is both

contrasted and identified with the world. This kind of equation was frequent, almost fashionable, in Hölderlin's age, but in Hölderlin—and specifically in *Hyperion*—it forms the backdrop for a fundamentally tragic view of life, of existence. The motto of the second part of *Hyperion* is the famous passage from Sophocles' *Oedipus at Colonus*: "Not to be born is, past all prizing, best; but, when a man has seen the light, this is next best by far, that with all speed he should go thither, whence he hath come."

But take care lest in your reading of *Hyperion* you attribute to it any of the romantic nostalgia for death that the Sophoclean motto is rightly felt to suggest. Hyperion does not solve his problem by killing himself or by getting killed (as a bona fide romantic hero—Werther, for instance—would have done). "Not even a beautiful dream," Hyperion says, "can prosper under the curse with which we are burdened." Not even the dream of death.

Our contemporary concern with Hölderlin—exceeding by far the timid interest granted him and his work by his contemporaries—emerges thus as somehow synonymous with the symptomatic significance of the existentialist curse. In other words, I suggest a lineage: Hölderlin, Kierkegaard, Heidegger, or if you will, Sartre. And if ever it seems a little "absurd" that existentialism—which badly strains the resources of philosophy, since it is ultimately not a philosophical but a poetic concern—has on its roster no name of a poet not hedged by excuses and qualifications, turn to Hölderlin.

A footnote to the foregoing: Having insisted that Hölderlin is not a poet of *Weltschmerz,* of romantic nostalgia for Greece or love or death, but simply and starkly a poet of the absolute tragic, we must note that there remains in his work one last vestige of tender unsublimated sentiment. One might go through all of *Hyperion* just watching for the word "child" to occur, and every time it does occur, one can be certain of sensing in it a remnant of sentimental hope. "In the child there is freedom." "In the child there is peace. . . . It is not yet at odds with itself." "I once saw a child put out its hand to catch the moonlight; but the light went calmly on its way. So do we stand trying to hold back ever-changing Fate." I sense that this residuum of sentimentality humanizes the cosmic tremor of the tragic.

IV

The closing words of Hyperion's forty-fifth and last letter to Bellarmin are: "More soon." This leaves the end of the work strangely open. Whatever we sense to be the import of these letters is not confined to the time of their composition. It is timeless. There could be, perhaps there were, more letters. We do not know how long the gods decreed the hermit's wait in Greece to last.

But "More soon" also suggests that Hölderlin himself could not believe that "the last word in the matter had been spoken." It hadn't.

The bibliography of *Hyperion* is unusually complex. A fragment of the novel, in a form never completed, was published in Schiller's periodical, *Neue Thalia,* in 1794. There is a manuscript of a metric version, which never progressed very far. There is a fragmentary manuscript of a third version entitled *Hyperion's Youth.* And there are three clearly distinct stages, extant in more or less complete form, of the work as it was published in 1797 and 1799. There are also, extant or reliably reported but not now traceable, manuscripts of Hyperion letters that the scholars charitably designate as belonging to a still later version and that were written in the course of Hölderlin's prolonged mental illness.

In a sense *Hyperion* never was finished. A poem is an

obsession from which the poet struggles to free himself. "One summer grant me, ye Mighty Ones," Hölderlin prayed, "one harvest time of ripened song." But the Mighty Ones did not grant his prayer.

To us *Hyperion* may be an ultimate achievement. To Hölderlin it was not the "ripened song" he wanted. Still less was his drama *Empedocles* in any of its multiple versions that "ripened song." And no one of his poems. He strove for a world. *"Du wolltest eine Welt."* He attempted the impossible. Had he succeeded, there would have been peace for him.

The poet's tragic struggle to achieve the impossible must be, in a strangely paradoxical way, a great source of encouragement to the translator. Willard Trask's English version of *Hyperion* is a superb accomplishment. But *Hyperion* is a poem; and one cannot *translate* poems, one can only *strive* to translate them. Willard Trask's English text is a more faithful rendering of Hölderlin's German than Hölderlin's published poem was of what could have given him peace. What greater praise can there be for a poetic translation?

I should like to say what specifically I see to be the merit of this translation. There is a popular and superficially appealing notion that a good translation reads as though it were an original composition. In this view the translator's mission is to present the foreign author as a domestic one, to clothe the foreign author in clothes the like of which the reader is used to seeing people wear.

There is a diametrically opposed conception, voiced most articulately by Ortega y Gasset. Here the argument is that the sole *raison d'être* of translation lies in its potential to enrich the translator's language and hence the culture with which that language is identified. Why translate, for example, Hölderlin's *Hyperion* into English if the result adds nothing to what the English reader has access to without it? The translator's mission is not to bring the foreign text to the reader but the reader to the foreign text.

But does it follow that a translation that gives the reader

the feeling that he is miraculously reading *Hyperion* in German, without ever having learned that language, must read unsmoothly at every turn? It does in the case of translators who have less than absolute artistic mastery of the language into which they translate. Mr. Trask's translation proves that the two principles of translation I have alluded to are not mutually exclusive.

ALEXANDER GODE-VON AESCH

PART ONE

Non coerceri maximo, contineri minimo, divinum est.

[NOT TO BE CONFINED BY THE GREATEST,
YET TO BE CONTAINED WITHIN THE SMALL-
EST, IS DIVINE.]

BOOK ONE

Hyperion to Bellarmin

Once again the dear soil of my native country brings me joy and sorrow.

Now every morning finds me on the heights of the Corinthian Isthmus; and often, like a bee among flowers, my soul flies back and forth between the seas that, to left and right, cool the feet of my glowing mountains.

One of the two gulfs would have delighted me especially, had I stood here a thousand years ago.

Then, surging on like a conquering demigod between the beautiful wilderness of Helicon and Parnassus where the red of dawn plays among a hundred snow-covered peaks, and the paradisal plain of Sicyon, the shining gulf undulated toward the city of joy, youthful Corinth, pouring out the captured wealth of every region before its favorite.

But what is that to me? The cry of the jackal, chanting his wild threnody amid the rubble of Antiquity, startles me from my dreams.

Fortunate the man whose native country flourishes to rejoice and strengthen his heart! For me, it is as if I were cast into a swamp, as if the coffin lid were being nailed shut over me, if anyone reminds me of mine, and whenever I hear myself called a Greek, it is as if I were being throttled with a dog collar.

And lo, my Bellarmin, often when such a remark escaped me, and perhaps anger brought a tear to my eye,

21

too, the knowing gentlemen who so much enjoy raising their voices among you Germans, and for whom a grieving heart makes the perfect opportunity to trot out their stale saws, lo, they were in their element, they presumed to tell me: "Do not complain, act!"

Oh that I had never acted! By how many hopes should I be the richer!—

Yes, only forget that there are men, O famished, beleaguered, infinitely troubled heart! and return thither whence you came, to the arms of Nature, the changeless, the quiet, the beautiful.

Hyperion to Bellarmin

I have nothing of which I may say that it is mine.

Distant and dead are my loved ones, and no voice brings me tidings of them more.

My business on earth is over and done. I set to work full of determination, I gave of my blood to it, and made the world not a penny the richer.

Unknown and alone, I have returned to wander through my native country, which lies about me like a vast graveyard; and perhaps what awaits me is the knife of the hunter who preserves us Greeks for his sport even as he does the wild beasts of the forest.

Yet still thou shinest, Sun of Heaven! Still dost thou grow green, sacred Earth! Still the rivers roar to the sea, and shady trees rustle under the noon of day. Spring's song of bliss sings my mortal thoughts to sleep. The fullness of the living universe feeds and satisfies my starving being with its intoxication.

O blessed Nature! I know not how it is with me when I raise my eyes to thy beauty, but all the joy of Heaven is in the tears that I weep in thy presence, beloved of beloveds!

My whole being falls silent and listens when the delicate swell of the breeze plays over my breast. Often, lost in the wide blue, I look up into the ether and down into the sacred sea, and I feel as if a kindred spirit were opening its arms to me, as if the pain of solitude were dissolved in the life of the Divinity.

To be one with all—this is the life divine, this is man's heaven.

To be one with all that lives, to return in blessed self-forgetfulness into the All of Nature—this is the pinnacle of thoughts and joys, this the sacred mountain peak, the place of eternal rest, where the noonday loses its oppressive heat and the thunder its voice and the boiling sea is as the heaving field of grain.

To be one with all that lives! At those words Virtue puts off her wrathful armor, the mind of man lays its scepter down, and all thoughts vanish before the image of the world in its eternal oneness, even as the striving artist's rules vanish before his Urania; and iron Fate renounces her dominion, and Death vanishes from the confederacy of beings, and indivisibility and eternal youth bless and beautify the world.

On this height I often stand, my Bellarmin. But an instant of reflection hurls me down. I reflect, and find myself as I was before—alone, with all the griefs of mortality; and my heart's refuge, the world in its eternal oneness, is gone; Nature closes her arms, and I stand like an alien before her and understand her not.

Ah! had I never gone to your schools! The knowledge which I pursued down its tunnels and galleries, from which, in my youthful folly, I expected the confirmation of all my pure joy—that knowledge has corrupted everything for me.

Among you I became so truly reasonable, learned so thoroughly to distinguish myself from what surrounds me, that now I am solitary in the beautiful world, an outcast from the garden of Nature, in which I grew and flowered, drying up under the noonday sun.

Oh, man is a god when he dreams, a beggar when he thinks; and when inspiration is gone, he stands, like a worthless son whom his father has driven out of the house, and stares at the miserable pence that pity has given him for the road.

Hyperion to Bellarmin

I thank you for asking me to tell you of myself, for making me remember earlier days.

What sent me back to Greece was wishing to live nearer to the places where I had played in my youth.

As the laborer into refreshing sleep, so my beleaguered being often sinks into the arms of the innocent past.

Peace of childhood! heavenly peace! how often do I pause before thee in loving contemplation, and fain would conceive thee! But our concepts are only of what has degenerated and been repaired; of childhood, of innocence we have no concept.

When I was still a child and in quietude, knowing nothing of all that is about us, was I not then more than now I am, after all my trouble of heart and all my thinking and struggling?

Yes, divine is the being of the child, so long as it has not been dipped in the chameleon colors of men.

The child is wholly what it is, and that is why it is so beautiful.

The pressure of Law and Fate touches it not; only in the child is freedom.

In the child is peace; it has not yet come to be at odds with itself. Wealth is in the child; it knows not its heart nor the inadequacy of life. It is immortal, for it has not heard of death.

But this men cannot bear. The divine must become like one of them, must learn that they, too, are there; and before Nature drives it out of its paradise, men entice and draw it out into the field of the curse, so that, like them, it shall drudge its life away in the sweat of its brow.

But the time of awakening is beautiful, too, if only we are not wakened unseasonably.

Oh, they are sacred days, in which our heart first tries its wings, in which, bursting with swift, fiery growth, we stand in the glorious world, like the young plant when it opens to the morning sun and stretches its tiny arms toward the infinite sky.

How was I driven then to the mountains, to the sea-shore! Ah, how often I sat with throbbing heart on the heights of Tina and watched the falcons and the cranes, and the bold, rejoicing ships as they vanished below the horizon! "There," I thought, "there beyond the horizon you too will one day wander"; and I felt as the man dying of thirst feels when he flings himself into the cooling current and splashes the foaming water over his face.

Then would I turn and go home, sighing. "If only," I often thought, "my school years were over!"

Innocent lad! They are still far from over.

That in his youth a man thinks the goal is so near! It is the most beautiful of all the illusions with which Nature supports the weakness of our being.

And often, as I lay there among the flowers, basking in the delicate spring light, and looked up into the serene blue that embraced the warm earth, when I sat under the elms and willows on the side of the mountain, after a re-freshing rain, when the branches were yet astir from the touch of the sky and golden clouds moved over the drip-ping woods; or when the evening star, breathing the spirit of peace, rose with the age-old youths and the other heroes of the sky, and I saw how the life in them moved on through the ether in eternal, effortless order, and the peace of the world surrounded and rejoiced me, so that I was suddenly alert and listening, yet did not know what was befalling me—"Dost thou love me, dear Father in Heaven," I whispered, and felt his answer so certainly and so blissfully in my heart.

O thou to whom I cried, as if thou wert above the stars, whom I named Maker of Heaven and Earth, kindly idol of my childhood, thou wilt not be wroth that I forgot thee!—Why is the world not poor enough to make us seek Another outside of it?*

Oh, if glorious Nature is the daughter of a Father, is not the daughter's heart his heart? Her inmost being, is

---

* It is scarcely necessary to say that no one can justly take offense at such expressions, which are no more than manifestations of a state of mind. [Hölderlin's note.]

it not He? But then, do I possess it? do I know it?

It is as if I saw, but afterward I am filled with fear again, as if what I saw had been my own shape; it is as if I felt it, the Spirit of the World, like a friend's warm hand, but I awake and think that I did but clasp my own finger.

Hyperion to Bellarmin

Do you know how Plato and his Stella loved each other?

So I loved, so was I loved. Oh, I was a fortunate lad!

It is pleasant when like and like meet in friendship; but it is divine when a great man draws littler men up to him.

A gracious word from a valiant heart, a smile under which the searing glory of the spirit hides itself, is little and is much, is like a magical password that conceals death and life in its simple syllable, is like living water that comes welling from the inmost recesses of the mountains, imparting the secret strength of the earth to us in its every crystal drop.

But how I hate all the barbarians who imagine that they are wise because there is no more heart left in them! all the self-important monstrosities who slay and desecrate beautiful youth a thousand times over with their dwarfing, meaningless discipline!

God in heaven! this is owls undertaking to drive eaglets from the nest and show them the way to the sun!

Forgive me, spirit of my Adamas, for mentioning these creatures before I speak of you. That is all the profit that we gain from experience—to be able to think of nothing excellent without thinking of its abortive opposite.

Oh! if only you were ever before me, with all that is akin to you, grieving demigod of whom I fondly think! He whom you, O warrior and champion, enfold in your stillness and strength, he whom you encounter with your love and wisdom—let him either run away or become like you! Meanness and weakness cannot survive beside you.

How often you were close to me when you were far from me and long had been, how often you illumined me with your light, warmed me so that my numbed heart moved again, like the frozen spring when heaven's ray touches it! Oh, how I wished I could flee among the stars with my happiness, that it might not be debased by what was around me!

I had grown up like a grapevine without a prop, the wild shoots trailed aimlessly over the ground. You know how many a noble power perishes in us because it is unused. I wandered like a will-o'-the-wisp, caught at everything, was caught by everything, but only for a moment; and my unskilled powers wore themselves out for nothing. I felt that everything failed me everywhere, yet I could not find my goal. Such was I when he found me.

He had long applied all his patience and his art to his material, the so-called cultivated world; but his material had been and had remained stone and wood, even if under compulsion it outwardly assumed the noble form of man; but that meant nothing to my Adamas. He wanted men, and he had found his art too poor to create them. Once upon a time they had existed, those whom he sought, those whom his art was too poor to create—this he knew for a certainty. Where they had existed he also knew. He resolved to go there and search under the rubble for their genius and thus to occupy his lonely days. He came to Greece. Such he was when I found him.

I can still see him come walking toward me, looking at me and smiling; I still hear his greeting and his questions.

As a man stands before a plant whose peace soothes his struggling spirit, and simple content returns to his soul —so he stood before me.

And I—was I not the echo of his quiet enthusiasm? did not the melodies of his being repeat themselves in me? What I saw, I became; and what I saw was divine.

How ineffectual is the best-intentioned diligence of men compared with the power of pure enthusiasm!

It does not stop at the surface, does not lay hold of us here or there, needs no time and no means, has no

use for command and coercion and persuasion; from all
sides, at every level of depth and height, it seizes us in-
stantly, and before we know it is there, before we can ask
what is befalling us, it transforms us through and through,
in all its beauty and bliss.

Well for him whom a noble spirit has thus encountered
in early youth!

Oh, those are golden, unforgettable days, filled with the
joys of love and sweet activity!

Soon did my Adamas lead me, now into Plutarch's
world of heroes, now into the magical land of the Greek
gods; now he quieted my youthful impatience with arith-
metic and geometry, now he climbed among the mountains
with me—by day for field flowers and woodland flowers
and the wild moss that grows on cliffs, by night that we
might gaze at the sacred stars above us, and understand
them as men may.

There is a precious sense of well-being in us when our
inner life thus draws strength from what is its material, dif-
ferentiates itself, and establishes truer inner relationships,
and our mind gradually comes of age to bear arms.

But with threefold force did I feel him and myself
when, like shades from a time long past, in pride and joy,
in rage and grief, we climbed Mount Athos and from there
sailed across to the Hellespont, then down to the shores
of Rhodes and the mountain gorges of Taenarum, through
all the quiet islands; when longing drove us from the coasts
inland to the somber heart of ancient Peloponnesus, to
the lonely banks of the Eurotas (ah! the valleys, lifeless
now, of Elis and Nemea and Olympia!); when, leaning
against a pillar of the temple of the forgotten Jupiter,
with oleander and periwinkle all around us, we gazed
into the wild riverbed, and the life of spring and the
ever-young sun bade us think that once man was there
and now is gone, that man's glorious nature, if it remains
there at all, remains but like a shattered fragment of a
temple, or only in memory, like the image of one dead—
and there I sat, playing sadly beside him, scraping the
moss from a demigod's pedestal, digging a marble hero's
shoulder out of the rubble, cutting the brambles and
heather from the half-buried architraves, while my

Adamas sketched the landscape that embraced the ruin, kindly and comforting: the wheat-covered hillock, the olive trees, the flock of goats hanging from the mountain's cliffs, the forest of elms dropping down from the peaks to the valley; and the lizard played at our feet and the flies buzzed about us in the silence of noon—Dear Bellarmin, I want to tell you of it all, point by point like Nestor; I move through the past like a gleaner over the stubblefield when the landowner has harvested; he gathers up every straw. And when I stood beside him on the heights of Delos, what a day it was that dawned for me as I climbed the ancient marble steps with him up the granite wall of Cynthus. Here once the Sun God dwelt, amid the divine festivals at which all Greece shone round him like a sky of golden clouds. Here the youth of Hellas plunged into full tides of joy and exaltation, as Achilles plunged into Styx, and came forth invincible as the demigod. In the groves, in the temples, their souls awoke and echoed musically in one another, and every youth faithfully guarded the treasure of that enchanting harmony.

But why do I speak of this? As if we still had even an inkling of those days! Oh, not even a beautiful dream can flourish under the curse that weighs upon us! Over the flowers of our spirit the present blows like a howling north-wind, blasting them even in the bud. And yet it was a golden day that wrapped me there on Cynthus! It was still gray dawn when we stood on the summit. Now he rose, the ancient Sun God, in his eternal youth; at peace and effortlessly as ever, the immortal Titan soared up with the thousand joys that are his, and smiled down on his devastated country, on his temples, his pillars, which fate had thrown down before him like withered rose petals that a child heedlessly tore from the branch as it passed and scattered over the ground.

"Be you like him!" Adamas cried, and grasped my hand and held it up toward the god; and it seemed to me that the winds of morning bore us along with them in the train of the divine being who now, in all his kindliness and greatness, rose to the summit of the heavens, and wondrously did his strength and his spirit fill us.

My inmost heart still mourns and rejoices over every word that Adamas spoke to me then; and I cannot understand how I can feel destitute, when I often feel as he must then have felt. What is loss, when a man finds himself in his own world? In us is all. Why should a man be miserable if a hair falls from his head? Why does he struggle so fiercely for servitude, when he could be a god? "You will be lonely, dear child!" This, too, Adamas said to me then. "You will be like the crane whose brothers leave him behind in the harsh time of the year, while they go to seek spring in a far country!"

And there it is, dear friend! It is this that makes us poor amid all wealth: that we cannot be alone, that, so long as we live, love does not perish in us. Give me my Adamas again, and come you with all who are akin to me, that the old, beautiful world may be renewed among us, that we may join together and be one in the arms of our divinity, Nature—and lo! I shall know nothing of lack.

But let no one tell me that Fate parts us! It is we, we ourselves! we delight in flinging ourselves into the night of the unknown, into the cold strangeness of any other world; if we could, we would leave the realm of the sun and rush headlong beyond the comet's track. Ah! for man's wild heart no home is possible; and as the sun's ray shrivels the very plants of earth that it has brought to bloom, so man kills the sweet flowers that flourish in his heart, the joys of kinship and love.

I seem to be chiding my Adamas for forsaking me, but I am not. Oh, he meant to come back!

A people of rare capacity is said to be hidden somewhere in the depths of Asia; thither his hope drove him.

I went with him as far as Nio. Those were bitter days. I have learned to bear pain, but I have no strength for such a parting.

With every moment that brought the last hour nearer, it became more apparent how deeply this man was woven into the very texture of my being. As one dying clings to his fleeing breath, so did my soul cling to him.

A few more days we passed at Homer's grave, and Nio became the most sacred of the islands to me.

Finally we tore ourselves away. My heart had struggled

until it was exhausted. I was calmer at the last moment.
I knelt before him, embraced him for the last time with
these arms. "Give me a blessing, my father," I cried softly
up to him, and he smiled; there was greatness in his smile,
his brow widened in the light of the morning stars, his
eye pierced the depths of the heavens—"Guard him
for me," he cried, "ye spirits of a better age! and draw
him up to your immortality; and all ye kindly powers of
Earth and Heaven, be with him!"

"There is a god in us," he added more quietly, "who
guides destiny as if it were a river of water, and all things
are his element. Above all else, may he be with you!"

So we parted. Farewell, my Bellarmin!

Hyperion to Bellarmin

Whither could I flee from myself, if I had not the sweet
days of my youth?

Like a shade that finds no rest by Acheron, I return
to the forsaken scenes of my life. All things age and
are rejuvenated. Why are we excepted from this beautiful
circling of Nature? Or does it rule us, too?

I should believe so, were it not for one trait that is in
us—the gigantic striving to be all things, which, like
Aetna's Titan, rages up from the depths of our being.

And yet, who would not rather feel it within him, like
seething oil, than acknowledge that he was born for the
whip and the yoke? A raging battlehorse, or a jade with
hanging ears—which is the nobler?

Dear friend! there was a time when my heart, too,
basked under the sun of great hopes, when the joy of immortality pulsed in my every vein, when I roved among
beautiful projects as through the half light of a vast forest,
when, happy as the fish in the sea in my shoreless future,
I pressed on, farther, ever farther.

How boldly, blessed Nature! did the youth leap from
thy cradle! how he rejoiced in his untried weapons! His
bow was drawn, his arrows rattled in the quiver, and the

immortals, the high spirits of Antiquity, led him on, and his Adamas was among them.

Wherever I went, wherever I stopped, their glorious presences were with me; in my thought the high deeds of all the ages were mingled together; and as those gigantic forms, the clouds of heaven, unite in one exultant storm, so the hundredfold victories of the Olympiads were united in me, so did they become one never-ending victory.

Who can abide it, whom does it not lay low, as a hurricane lays low young woods, when the terrifying splendor of Antiquity seizes him as it seized me, when, as for me, the surroundings are lacking in which he might gain a strengthening self-reliance?

Oh, as for me, the greatness of the ancients bowed my head like a storm, swept the bloom from my face; and often I lay where no eye saw me, weeping a thousand tears, as a fallen fir tree lies by a stream and hides its faded crown in the water. How gladly would I have paid with blood for one moment from the life of a great man!

But what use was that? No one wanted me, no one!

Oh, it is pitiful to see oneself so reduced to nothing; and let him who does not understand this ask no more but give thanks to Nature who made him, like the butterflies, for joy; let him go and never in his lifetime speak again of pain and mischance.

I loved my heroes as a fly loves the light; I sought their perilous presence, and fled, and sought it again.

As a bleeding stag plunges into the stream, so I often plunged into the whirlpool of pleasures, to cool my burning breast and wash away the raging, glorious dreams of fame and greatness; but what use was that?

And when, as often toward midnight, my hot heart drove me down into the garden under the dewy trees, and the lullaby of the fountain and the sweet air and the moonlight soothed my thought, and the silver clouds moved in such freedom and peace above me, and from far away the fading voice of the sea came faintly, oh! then how graciously did all the great phantoms that it loved play with my heart!

"Farewell, ye heavenly spirits!" I often said in thought, when above me the melody of the dawn's light began softly sounding. "Ye glorious dead, farewell! Would that I could follow you, would that I could cast off all that my century has given me, and make my way into the freer realm of the shades!"

But I languish on the chain and snatch with bitter joy the miserly bowl that is offered to my thirst.

Hyperion to Bellarmin

My island had become too cramped for me, now that Adamas was gone. For years, in fact, Tina had held nothing for me but tedium. I determined to go out into the world.

"Go to Smyrna first," said my father; "master the arts of navigation and war there, learn the speech of polished peoples and their political constitutions, their views, their manners and customs, investigate everything, and choose the best!—Go on from there, if you will."

"Learn a little patience, too," my mother added, and I accepted the advice gratefully.

To take the first step beyond the circle of youth is pure enchantment; it is as if I were thinking of my birthday when I think of my departure from Tina. There was a new sun above me, and land and sea and air had a new relish, as if I were enjoying them for the first time.

The ardor and activity with which I now pursued my education in Smyrna, and my speedy progress, did not a little to calm my heart. And I remember, too, many a blissful holiday evening from that time. How often I walked under the ever green trees on the bank of the Meles, by the birthplace of my Homer, and picked an offering of flowers and cast them into the sacred stream! Then in my peaceful dreams I approached the nearby grotto where, they say, the old man sang his Iliad. I found him. Every sound in me was stilled by his presence. I opened his divine poem, and it was as if I had never known it, so differently did it now come to life in me.

I like to remember, too, my wanderings through the countryside about Smyrna. It is a radiant land, and a thousand times I have wished I had wings, that once a year I might fly to Asia Minor.

From the plain of Sardis I climbed up the rock defiles of Tmolus.

I had spent the night in a hospitable hut at the foot of the mountain, among myrtles and the scent of the labdanum-bearing cistus, where in the golden stream of Pactolus the swans played beside me, where an ancient temple of Cybele looked out from the elms into the clear moonlight like a shy ghost. Five lovely pillars mourned over the rubble, and a kingly portal lay fallen at their feet.

Now my path waxed upward through a thousand blossoming shrubs. Whispering trees leaned down from the rugged slope, dropping their delicate floss on my head. I had set out with the morning. By noon I reached the summit of the mountain. I stood, looking happily about me, relishing the purer airs of the sky. They were blessed hours.

Like a sea, the countryside from which I had climbed up lay spread before me, youthful, filled with living joy; spring's heavenly, unending play of colors greeted my heart; and, even as the Sun in the heavens found himself again in the thousand changes of light that the Earth sent back to him, so my spirit recognized itself in the fullness of life that was all about it, that beset it from every side.

To the left the stream, an exulting giant, plunged down into the woods from the marble cliff that hung over me, where the eagle played with his fledglings, where the snow-crowned peaks glittered up into the blue ether; to the right storm clouds came rolling over the forests of Sipylus; I did not feel the rushing wind that bore them on, I felt only a faint breeze in my hair; but I heard their thunder as we hear the voice of the future, and I saw their flames, like the distant light of dimly apprehended divinity. I turned southward and walked on. Now there lay before me the whole paradisal countryside through which the Caystrus flows in so many an enchanting meander, as if

imágens ge

it could not linger long enough amid the profusion and loveliness that surrounds it. Like the zephyrs, my spirit wandered blissfully from beauty to beauty, from unknown, peaceful villages lying deep at the foot of the mountain, on to where the chain of Messogis was dimly visible.

I came back to Smyrna like a drunken man from a feast. My heart was too full of pleasant things not to impart some of its abundance to mortal existence; Nature had yielded me too happy a booty of her loveliness for me not to make good the deficiencies of human life with it. My paltry Smyrna clad herself in the colors of my enthusiasm and stood before me like a bride. Her flocking citizens attracted me. The absurdity of their ways amused me like a children's prank; and since by nature I was above their established forms and customs, I played with them all, putting them on and taking them off like carnival costumes.

But what I now found giving some savor to the insipid fare of daily intercourse was the well-proportioned faces and figures that compassionate Nature still sends, here and there, like stars into our darkness.

What heartfelt pleasure I took in them! With what faith did I read those smiling hieroglyphics! But I had almost the same experience with them that I had had long ago with birches in spring. I had heard of the sap of these trees and was all agog at the thought of what a precious drink their graceful stems must yield. But there was neither strength nor life enough in it.

And, oh! how irredeemably wanting was everything else that I heard and saw!

As I went now here, now there among these polished people, it seemed to me that human nature had resolved itself into the multifarious species of the animal kingdom. As everywhere, so here, too, the men were especially demoralized and corrupted.

Some animals howl when they hear music. But my more mannerly humans laughed when the conversation turned to beauty of spirit and virtue of heart. Wolves run away when you strike a light. When these men saw a spark of reason, they turned their backs like thieves.

If ever I happened to say a warm word for ancient

Greece, they yawned and let it be known that after all a man had to live in this day and age; and—someone else added sententiously—good taste had not perished from the earth.

And so I saw: one would crack jokes like a sailor, another puffed out his cheeks and delivered old saws.

Yet another, to demonstrate what an advanced thinker he was, would snap his fingers at Heaven and cry that he had never worried about the birds in the bush, give him birds in the hand! Yet when death was mentioned before him, he would at once clasp his hands, and as the conversation went on, would manage to put in that it was a very dangerous thing that our priests no longer had any influence.

The only people from whom I sometimes profited were the storytellers, the living gazettes of foreign cities and countries, the speaking peep-boxes in which one can see potentates on chargers and church steeples and markets.

At last I grew weary of wasting myself, of looking for grapes in the desert and flowers on a glacier.

I now lived more determinedly alone, and the sweet spirit of my youth had almost vanished from my heart. The incurable corruption of my century became so apparent to me from so many things that I tell you and do not tell you, and my beautiful faith that I would find my world in *one* soul, that I would embrace my whole kind in *one* sympathetic being—that, too, forsook me.

Dear friend! What would life be without hope? A spark that leaps from a coal and goes out, a blast of wind in the dreary time of the year, heard for a moment and then still forever—would it be so with us?

Even the swallow seeks a more hospitable country in winter, the wild beasts run hither and yon in the heat of the day, their eyes search for the stream.

Who tells the babe that its mother will not deny it the breast? And yet it seeks for it!

Nothing would live if it did not hope. My heart now shut away its treasures, but only to keep them safe for a better time, for the unique, the sacred revelation of fidelity that surely, at some epoch of my existence, would come to my thirsting soul.

How blissfully I often cleaved to it when, in hours of veiled foreseeing, it played about me softly as moonlight, soothing my brow. Even then I knew you; even then, maiden, you looked down at me from the clouds like a Genius—you who in time to come rose before me out of the turbid sea of the world in all the peace of beauty! Then this heart struggled and burned no more.

As a lily sways in newly stilled air, so my being moved in its element, in my ravishing dreams of her.

Hyperion to Bellarmin

Smyrna had lost all attraction for me now. Altogether, my heart had grown gradually wearier. At moments, to be sure, the wish could still take me to travel through the world, or to turn soldier and fight in some war, or to find my Adamas and burn my discontent to ashes in his fire; but that was as far as it ever went, and my meaningless, parched life refused to be renewed.

Soon summer was over; in feeling, I already anticipated the sullen days of rain, and the whistling winds, and the roar of storm-swollen streams; and Nature, which had surged up into every plant and tree like a foaming fountain, now stood before my darkened apprehension fading and closed and turned in upon itself, even as I was.

Yet I wanted to take with me what I could of all this fleeing life; everything outward to which I had become attached, I wanted to preserve within me, for I knew well that the returning year would not find me among these trees and mountains; so now I walked and rode more than ever before through all the countryside.

But what most impelled me to go out was my secret longing to see a man whom for some little time I had come upon every day when I passed under the trees outside the city gate.

Like a young Titan, this noble stranger strode resplendent among that race of dwarfs, who fed upon his beauty in joyous dread, measured his tall stature and his strength, and with covert glances regaled themselves on the Roman majesty of his shining face, as upon forbidden fruit. And it was a glorious moment each time that this man's eye, for whose glance the ether seemed too narrow, put off all pride and searched until, with an effort, it found its way to mine and, blushing, we gazed after each other and passed on.

One day I had ridden deep into the forest on Mount Mimas and did not start back until late in the evening. I had dismounted and was leading my horse down a steep, wild path, over tree roots and stones. As I was thus making my way through the underbrush into the gulf that now opened before me, a pair of Karaborniote robbers suddenly fell on me, and for a moment I was hard put to it to ward off the two drawn sabers; but they were already tired from other work, so I managed. I quietly mounted my horse again and rode on.

At the foot of the mountain, between woods and soaring cliffs, a little meadow opened before me. It grew light. The moon had just risen over the dark trees. Some distance away I saw horses lying stretched out and men beside them on the grass.

"Who are you?" I cried.

"That is Hyperion!" cried a voice that rang like a hero's, in happy surprise. "You know me," the voice continued; "I see you every day under the trees outside the city gate."

My horse flew to him like an arrow. The moon shone bright on his face. I recognized him; I sprang to the ground.

"Good evening!" he cried, charming in his youthful vigor, and looked at me with his wild eyes subdued to tenderness, while his sinewy hand grasped mine so that the touch of it penetrated to my inmost being.

Oh! now my meaningless life was at an end!

Alabanda (such was the stranger's name) now told me that he and his servant had been set upon by robbers, that the two I had come upon had been sent about their business by him, that he had missed the path out of the woods, and so had been obliged to stay where he was until I arrived. "It has cost me a friend," he added, and pointed to his dead horse.

I turned mine over to his servant, and he and I set out together on foot.

"It served us right," I began, as, arm in arm, we made our way out of the wood; "why did we hesitate so long and pass each other by, until misfortune brought us together?"

"But it was you, I must tell you," answered Alabanda, "who were most to blame, you were the colder. I rode after you today."

"Noble youth!" I cried, "wait and see! You shall never surpass me in love!"

We became ever more intimate and happier together.

Near to the city we passed a well-built caravansary, set peacefully among murmuring brooks and fruit trees and sweet-scented meadows. We decided to spend the night there. For a long time we sat on together by the open window. The high silence of spirit enveloped us. Earth and ocean was blissfully silent, like the stars that hung above us. It was much if even a breeze flitted into the room from the sea and played delicately with the candle, or if the stronger tones of more distant music penetrated to us, while the thunderclouds lulled themselves to sleep in the bed of the ether, now and again to sound distantly, as a sleeping giant breathes more heavily in his dread dreams.

Our souls were impelled toward each other all the more strongly because they had come together against our will. We met like two brooks that, pouring from a mountain, fling off their burden of earth and stone and rotten wood and the whole sluggish chaos that holds them back, determined to clear the way to each other, to burst through until, clasping and clasped with equal force, they set out, mingled in one majestic stream, on their long journey to the sea.

He, driven by fate and human barbarity from his own home to wander among strangers, embittered and unguided from early youth, and yet with his inmost heart full of love, full of longing to break out of the coarse husk and win through into a congenial element; I, already so profoundly cut off from everything, so utterly and determinedly a stranger and alone among men, with the most precious melody of my heart so absurdly accompanied by all the world's tinkling bells; I, the scorn and aversion of all the lame and the blind, and yet in my own judgment only too lame and blind, so intolerably burdensome to myself by everything in me that was even distantly akin to worldly wisdom and pseudo-reason, to the barbarians and the would-be wits—and so full of hope, so single-mindedly awaiting but one thing, a more beautiful life—

Was it not inevitable that these two youths should embrace each other in such joyous and impetuous haste?

O my friend and brother-in-arms, my Alabanda! where are you? Almost I believe that you have made your way to the unknown land, to rest, have become again what once we were as children.

Sometimes, when a storm passes over me, dispensing its divine powers among woods and sown fields alike, or when the waves of the sea play together, or a choral train of eagles soars about the mountain peaks among which I am wandering, my heart can stir as if my Alabanda were not far away. But more visibly, more presently, more unmistakably does he live in me—the whole man —as once he stood, stern and aglow and terrible, denouncing the sins of this century. How my spirit awoke in its depths! how the thundering words of implacable justice rolled on my tongue! Like messengers of Nemesis, our thoughts journeyed over the whole earth, purifying it until no trace of a curse remained.

We summoned the past, too, before our bar of justice, and proud Rome did not cow us with its splendor nor Athens corrupt us with its youthful bloom.

As storms, exulting in their unwearied play, travel on through forests, over mountains, so our souls drove ever forward in colossal projects—not that we effeminately created our world as by a magic spell and, childishly inexperienced, expected no resistance; Alabanda was too intelligent and too brave for that. But even spontaneous enthusiasm is often militant and shrewd.

One day is especially present to me.

We had gone to the country together and were sitting with our arms trustfully around each other in the dark shade of an ever green laurel, looking at our Plato—the passage where he speaks with such wondrous sublimity of aging and rejuvenation; from time to time we rested, looking out over the mute, leafless landscape, where the sky, playing with clouds and sunlight, was more than ever beautiful among the autumnally sleeping trees.

We then spoke much of Greece as it is today, both of us with bleeding hearts, for the desecrated soil was Alabanda's native country too.

Alabanda was moved to a degree most unusual in him.

"When I see a child," he cried, "and think how shameful and stultifying is the yoke that it will bear, and that it will starve as we do, look for men as we do, search after truth and beauty as we do, will waste away in barren pining because it is alone as we are, that it— O men of this land! take your sons from the cradle and cast them into the river, that at least they will be spared your ignominy!"

"Surely, Alabanda," said I, "surely, it will not always be so."

"What can change it?" he answered. "Our heroes have lost their fame, our wise men their pupils. Great deeds, when there is no noble people to understand them, are no more than a powerful blow on an unresponsive brow, and high words, when they do not echo in high hearts, are like a dying leaf rustling down onto dung. What are you going to do?"

"I will take a shovel and throw the dung into a pit. A people among whom spirit and greatness no longer engenders any spirit and any greatness has nothing in common with other peoples who are still men, has no more rights; and it is an empty farce, sheer superstition, to go on honoring such will-less corpses as if a Roman heart beat in them. Away with them! The withered, decaying tree shall not stand where it stands, it steals light and air from the young life that is ripening for a new world!"

Alabanda flew to me and embraced me, and his kisses penetrated to my soul. "Companion in the fight!" he cried, "dear brother! oh, now I have a hundred arms!

"I have heard my melody at last," he continued, in a

voice that stirred my heart like a battle cry; "it is enough! You have spoken a glorious word, Hyperion. What! shall the god be dependent upon the worm? The god in us, for whose road infinity lies open—shall he stand and wait until the worm crawls out of his way? No! no! We do not ask if you are willing, you serfs and barbarians! You are never willing! Nor will we try to make you better, for that is useless! We will but make certain that you get out of the way of humanity's victorious career! Oh! let some-one light a torch for me, that I may burn the weeds from the field, let someone lay me the mine with which I can blow the dull clods from the face of the earth!"

"When possible, we should but gently push them aside," I interrupted.

Alabanda was silent for a while.

"I find my joy in the future," he began again at last, and ardently seized both my hands. "Thank God, I shall come to no common end! To be happy means to be sleepy, in the language of slaves. Happiness! it is as if I had pap and lukewarm water in my mouth when they talk to me of happiness. So vapid and so irredeemable is all for which you slaves give up your laurel crowns, your immortality!

"Oh, holy light, which, moving tirelessly above us, fills all its immense realm with its power and imparts its soul even unto me in the rays that I drink—may thy bliss be mine!

"The children of the sun live by their deeds; they live by victory; their own spirit rouses them, and their strength is their joy."

The spirit of this man often laid hold of me with such force that I might well have felt ashamed of being snatched up and carried away like any feather.

"O Heaven and Earth!" I cried, "this is joy!—This is another age, this is no voice from my infantile century, this is not the soil on which the heart of man pants under the oppressor's whip.—Yes, yes, by your glorious soul, O man! you will save my fatherland!"

"So I will," he cried, "or perish."

From that day on we became ever more sacred, ever dearer to each other. A gravity of purpose that was indescribably profound had arisen between us. Each of us lived only in the eternal fundamental tones of his being, and we moved austerely from one great harmony to another. Our life together was filled with glorious sternness and courage.

"Whatever has made you so tongue-tied?" Alabanda once smilingly asked me. "In the tropical regions, nearer the sun," said I, "the birds do not sing either."

But everything is now up, now down in this world; and man, for all his gigantic powers, holds nothing fast. I once saw a child put out its hand to catch the moonlight; but the light went calmly on its way. So do we stand trying to hold back ever-changing Fate.

Oh, that it were possible but to watch it as peacefully and meditatively as we do the circling stars!

The happier one is, the less it takes to destroy one; and such blissful days as Alabanda and I were living are like a steep crag where your traveling companion has but to touch you to fling you involuntarily down over the jagged edge into the lightless depths.

We had made a glorious voyage to Chios, had found a thousand joys in each other. Like breezes over the plain of the sea, the kindly enchantment of Nature had played about us. We looked at each other in happy surprise, without speaking, but our eyes said: I have never seen you like this. So gloriously transfigured were we by the powers of Earth and Heaven.

We had argued, too, gaily and ardently, over many things during the voyage; as so often before, I had taken the most heartfelt delight in watching that spirit on its bold, erratic course, following its path in such unconstrained gladness yet for the most part so unfalteringly.

No sooner had we landed than we hastened to be alone.

"You cannot persuade anyone," I cried with fondest love; "you convince men, you win them over, before you begin. When you speak, none can doubt; and he who does not doubt is not persuaded."

"Proud flatterer!" he cried in answer. "You lie! But you have given me a timely reminder. Only too often have you made me forsake reason! Not for the world and all its crowns would I be freed of you, but it often troubles me that you are so indispensable to me, that I am so bound to you. And since," he continued, "you possess me so entirely, it is time that you knew me entirely! Amid all these splendors and all our joys, we have not thought of looking back at the past."

And he told me the story of his life; and I felt as if I were watching a young Hercules battling with Megaera.

"Now will you forgive me," he ended the tale of his adversities, "will you take it more calmly if I am often harsh and offensive and intolerable?"

"Say it not!" I cried, moved to the depths; "it is wonder enough that you are still here, that you kept yourself alive for me!"

"Yes, for you!" he cried, "and it rejoices my heart that I am still a palatable dish for you. And if I sometimes taste like a crab apple to you, squeeze me in the press until I am fit to drink."

"Let me be! let me be!" I cried; I strove in vain, the man turned me into a child, and I could not hide it from him; he saw my tears, and woe to him if he had not the right to see them!

"We are rioting in pleasures," Alabanda began again; "we are wasting time in drunkenness."

"We are celebrating our betrothal," I cried gaily, "it is only right that it should sound as if we were in Arcadia. —But to return to what we were talking of earlier!

"You accord the state far too much power. It must not demand what it cannot extort. But what love gives, and spirit, cannot be extorted. Let the state leave that alone, or we will take its laws and whip them in the pillory! By Heaven! he knows not what his sin is who would make the state a school of morals. The state has always been made a hell by man's wanting to make it his heaven.

"The state is the coarse husk around the seed of life, and nothing more. It is the wall around the garden of human fruits and flowers.

"But is the wall around the garden of any help when the soil lies parched? Only the rain from heaven helps then.

"O rain from heaven! O enthusiasm! thou wilt bring us the springtime of peoples again. The state cannot com-

mand thy presence. But let it not obstruct thee, and thou
wilt come, come with thine all-conquering ecstasies, wilt
wrap us in golden clouds and carry us up above this
mortal world; and we shall marvel and wonder if this is
still we, we who in our poverty asked the stars if a spring
bloomed for us among them.—Do you ask me when
this will be? It will be when the darling of Time, the
youngest, loveliest daughter of Time, the new Church,
will arise out of these polluted, antiquated forms, when
the awakened feeling of the divine will bring man his
divinity, man's heart its beautiful youth again, when—
I cannot prophesy it, for my eyes are too dim to surmise
it, but it will come, that I know for certain. Death is a
messenger of life, and that we now lie asleep in our in-
firmaries testifies that we shall soon awaken to new health.
Then, and not till then, shall we exist, then, then will our
spirit's element have been found!"

Alabanda was silent and gazed at me for a moment in
astonishment. I was carried away by boundless hopes;
divine forces bore me on like a summer cloud—

"Come!" I cried and grasped his garment, "come! who
can any longer abide in the prison that darkens around
us?"

"Come where, my enthusiast?" Alabanda answered
drily, and a shadow of mockery seemed to pass over his
face.

I was as if fallen from the clouds. "Go!" I said, "you
are a man of naught!"

At that moment some strangers entered the room. They
were striking figures, haggard and pale for the most part,
so far as I could see by the moonlight, and calm; but
there was something in their countenances that pierced the
soul like a sword, and it was as if one were standing in
the presence of omniscience; one would have doubted that
this was the outward form of creatures subject to needs,
if here and there slain emotion had not left its traces.

One of them struck me especially. The stillness of his
features was the stillness of a battlefield. Wrath and love
had raged in this man, and understanding shone over the
wreckage of feeling like the eye of a hawk perched upon
ruined palaces. Profound contempt was on his lips. One

felt that this man was bent upon no insignificant purpose.

Another appeared to owe his calm rather to a natural hardness of heart. He showed almost no trace of violence perpetrated either by his own will or by Fate.

A third seemed rather to have wrested his coldness from life by the force of his conviction, and still to be often at odds with himself; for there was a concealed contradiction in his being, and I thought that he had to keep a tight rein on himself. Of them all, he spoke the least.

As they entered, Alabanda sprang up like bent steel.

"We have been seeking you," one cried.

"You would find me," he said with a laugh, "if I were hidden at the center of the earth. They are my friends," he added, turning to me.

They seemed to scrutinize me with a certain severity.

"He, too, is one of those who would see the world a better place," Alabanda cried after a moment, and pointed to me.

"Are you serious in this?" one of the three asked me.

"It is no joking matter to better the world," said I.

"You have said much in little!" cried one. "You are our man!" added another.

"Are you of the same mind as I?" I asked.

"Ask what we are doing," came the answer.

"And if I asked?"

"We would tell you we are here to purge the earth, that we clear the stones from the field and break up the hard clods with the mattock and draw furrows with the plow, that we grasp the rank growth by the roots, cut it through at the roots, and tear it up by the roots, so that it shall wither in the burning sun."

"Not that we may reap," another interrupted; "the reward of our labors will come too late for us; the harvest will not ripen in our time.

"We are at the evening of our days. We often went wrong, we hoped much and did little. We ventured rather than deliberated. We were eager to have done and trusted to luck. We spoke much of joy and sorrow and loved and hated them both. We played with fate, and fate with us. It tossed us high and low, from beggar's staff to crown. It swung us as one swings a glowing censer, and we glowed until the coals turned to ashes. We have ceased to speak of good and evil fortune. We have grown beyond the midpoint of life, where it is green and warm. But it is not the worst in man that outlives youth. The cold sword is forged from hot metal. They say that grapes grown on burned-out, dead volcanoes yield no bad must."

"We say this not for our sake," another now cried in more hurried tones, "but for yours! We do not go begging for men's hearts. For we need neither their hearts nor their wills. For men are in no case against us, since everything is for us, and the fools and the cunning, the simple and the wise, and all the vices and virtues of incivility and good breeding are at our service without hire and blindly help us on toward our goal—we only hope that some might be found to know the joy of it, and so, among our thousand blind helpers, we choose out the best, that we may make them into seeing helpers—but if no one wants to live where we have built, it is neither our fault nor our loss. We did what was for us to do. If no one wants to reap where we plowed, who can blame us for that? Who upbraids the tree when its fruit falls into the mire? I have often said to myself, 'You are sacrificing to decay,' and yet I finished my day's work."

"These are traitors!" the very walls dinned into my sensitive heart. I felt like one suffocating in smoke, breaking open doors and windows to escape—so did I thirst for air and freedom.

They soon saw, too, how uneasy I felt, and broke off. Day was already dawning when I stepped out of the caravansary where we had been together. I felt the morning breeze like balsam on a burning wound.

I was already too irritated by Alabanda's mockery not to be completely confused by his having these mysterious friends.

"He is evil," I cried, "yes, evil! He feigns unbounded trust, and consorts with such as these—and hides it from you!"

I felt like a girl who learns that her betrothed is secretly living with a whore.

Oh, it was not the grief that one can cherish, that one

carries in one's heart like a child, that sings in sleep with the voice of the nightingale!

Like a raging snake that, gliding implacably up legs and loins to coil round every limb, sinks its poisonous fangs now into its victim's chest, now into his back—so it held me in its terrible embrace. I summoned all the courage of my heart to my aid, and struggled for noble thoughts, that I might remain calm; for a few moments I succeeded, but now I had gained strength enough for fury, and now, as if it were arson, I killed every spark of love in me.

"He must," I thought, "yes—for these are his friends—he must be conspiring with them against you! But what did he want with you? What could he have been trying to get from you and your enthusiasm? Oh, had he but gone his way! But these people have a strange desire to take up with their opposite! to have some queer animal in their stable suits them to perfection!"—

And yet I had been unspeakably happy with him, had so often sunk into his embraces only to awaken from them with my heart invincible, had so often been hardened and refined in his fire like steel!

On one serene midnight, when I pointed out the Dioscuri to him, Alabanda laid his hand on my heart and said: "These are but stars, Hyperion, by which the name of the heroic brothers is written in the sky; but *they* are in us, living and true, with their courage and their divine love, and you! you are the son of a God and share your immortality with your mortal Castor!"—

When once I wandered through the forests of Ida with him, and we made our way down into the valley that we might ask the silent grave mounds there to tell us of their dead, and I said to Alabanda that one among them might perhaps belong to the spirit of Achilles and his beloved, and Alabanda confided to me that he was often childish enough to think that we would fall together in one battle-torn valley and rest together under one tree—who then would have thought what was to come?

I reflected with all the power of thought that remained to me, I accused him, defended him, accused him again all the more bitterly; I struggled against my mood, de-

termined to be cheerful, and thereby only plunged myself
in blackest darkness.

Ah! my eye was already so sore from many a blow,
was only just beginning to heal—how could it see more
healthily now?

Alabanda visited me the next day. My heart boiled
when he entered, but I controlled myself, however much
his pride and imperturbability agitated and infuriated me.

"The air is glorious," he said at last, "and it will be a
rarely beautiful evening; let us go up to the Acropolis
together!"

I accepted. For a long time we said not a word. "What
do you want?" I at last asked.

"Can you ask me that?" the tameless youth answered,
with a melancholy that pierced my soul. I was stricken,
bewildered.

"What am I to think of you?" I began again at last.

"What I am," he answered calmly.

"You must clear yourself," I said in a changed voice,
and looked at him proudly, "clear yourself! absolve yourself!"

That was too much for him.

"How comes it," he cried indignantly, "that this fellow
can twist me as he pleases?—True enough, I was turned
out of school too early. I had dragged all chains and I
had broken them, only one remained, only one was still
to be snapped, I had not yet been chided by a weathercock
of a fellow—stop your muttering, I have kept silent long
enough!"

"O Alabanda, Alabanda," I cried.

"Be still," he answered; "and use not my name as a
dagger against me."

Now anger raged uncontrolled in me, too. We did not
rest until any turning back was well-nigh impossible.
We violently destroyed the garden of our love. Often we
stopped and stood silent, and oh so gladly, so joyously
would we have fallen on each other's necks; but accursed
pride stifled every tone of love that rose from our hearts.

"Farewell!" I cried at last, and rushed away. But against
my will I looked back, and against his will Alabanda had
followed me.

"A strange beggar, is he not, Alabanda?" I cried; "he throws his last penny into the bog!"

"If he does, then let him go hungry!" he cried, and left me.

I staggered away, stupefied. Then I was standing by the sea, gazing at the waves—ah! it was beneath them that my heart longed to be, there beneath them, and my arms flew toward the unfettered tide; but soon, as if from heaven, a gentler spirit came over me and restrained my unruly, sorrowing heart with its peaceable rod; more tranquilly now, I reflected on the course of my life, my belief in the world, my cheerless experiences, I considered men, as I had felt them and known them from my early youth, men of the most various upbringing, and everywhere I found but false notes, muffled or strident; only in the simple confines of the child did I find pure melodies— "It is better," I said to myself, "to become as the bee and build one's house in innocence, than to rule with the masters of the world and howl with them as with wolves, than to dominate peoples and befoul one's hands with that unclean material." I wanted to go back to Tina and live for my gardens and fields.

Smile if you will! I was utterly serious. If the life of the world consists in an alternation between opening and closing, between going forth and returning, why is it not even so with the heart of man?

To be sure, I found this new lesson hard to accept; to be sure, I was loth to turn from the error of my youth—who gladly tears off his wings?—but it was what must be!

I went through with it. I took ship. A fresh wind from the mountains drove me out of the harbor of Smyrna. In a miraculous peace, exactly like a child that knows nothing of the instant to come, I lay in my bark and gazed at the trees and mosques of the city, my eyes traced my green walks along the shore, the path by which I climbed the Acropolis, I saw them and let them go, recede farther and farther; but now, as I came out into the open sea, and everything slowly sank down behind me, like a coffin into a grave, suddenly it was as if my heart had broken— "O Heaven!" I cried, and all the life in me awoke and strove to hold back the fleeing present, but it was gone, gone!

Like a mist it lay before me, the divine land where, like a roebuck free of the meadow, I had wandered far and wide through valleys and mountains, and brought the echo of my heart to springs and streams, to the distances and depths of the earth.

There inland I had climbed Tmolus in solitary innocence; down there where Ephesus once stood in its happy youth and Teos and Miletus, up there in the sacred, mourning Troad, I had wandered with Alabanda, with Alabanda! and there like a god I had ruled him, and like a tender, confiding child I had obeyed his eye in joy of soul, with the most intense delight in his being, always happy, whether I held his horse for him or, carried above myself, I met his soul in glorious resolves, in daring thoughts, in the fire of eloquence!

And now it was all over, now I was nothing, now I had been so irremediably deprived of everything, had become the poorest of men, and did not myself know how.

"O eternal labyrinth!" I thought, "when will man escape from thy thralldom?"

We speak of our hearts, of our plans, as if they were ours; yet there is a power outside of us that tosses us hither and thither as it pleases until it lays us in the grave, and of which we know not whence it comes nor whither it is bound.

We want to grow upward, and spread wide our branches and twigs, yet soil and weather bring us to whatever is to be, and when the lightning strikes your crown and splits you to the roots, poor tree! what part have you in it?

So I thought. Are you displeased, my Bellarmin? There is yet more that you must hear.

The sad thing, dear friend, is that our mind so eagerly assumes the posture of our erring heart, so fondly clings to passing grief; that thought, which should heal sorrows, itself sickens; that the gardener, charged with planting rose-bushes, so often tears his hand on them—oh! this has made a fool of many a man before others whom, but for this, he would have ruled like an Orpheus, this has so

often made the noblest nature a laughingstock to such
fellows as can be found in every street, this is the hidden
reef for the favored of Heaven—that their love is strong
and tender like their spirit, that their hearts are often
stirred to motions swifter and more impetuous than the
waves that the God of the Sea governs with his trident.
Wherefore, my friend, let none be proud!

Hyperion to Bellarmin

Can you listen, will you understand, if I tell you of my
long sickness of grief?

Accept me as I present myself, and consider that it
is better to die because one has lived than to live because
one never lived! Envy not the carefree, the wooden images
who want nothing because their souls are so lacking in
everything, who do not ask if the sun will shine or the
rain fall, because they have nothing to cultivate.

Yes, yes! it is very easy indeed to be happy and at
peace, with a shallow heart and a narrow mind. Let them
enjoy it; who goes into a passion if the wooden target
does not cry woe when the arrow strikes it, if the empty
pot gives such a hollow sound when someone throws it
against the wall?

Only, dear people, you must resign yourselves, and hold
your tongues and wonder, if you cannot understand that
others are not so happy as you are nor so self-satisfied;
you must beware of making your wisdom law, for obedience to you would be the end of the world.

I was now living very quietly and unpretentiously in
Tina. I really succeeded in letting the shows of the world
pass by like mists in autumn; often, too, I laughed—
though with tears in my eyes—at my heart, when it went
flying off to regale itself like the bird that pecks at painted
grapes, yet withal I remained unsoured and unperturbed.

I grudged no one his opinions or his improprieties. I
was converted, I no longer wished to convert others; it
only saddened me when I saw that people believed that

I did not interfere with their clownish behavior because I esteemed it as highly as they did. I was not willing actually to subject myself to their nonsense, but I tried to let it pass wherever I could. "It is all the pleasure they have," I thought, "it is their life!"

Often I was even pleased to join in with them; yet, however apathetically and unspontaneously I made the effort, not one of them ever noticed, not one of them was aware of any lack in me, and had I asked them to excuse me, they would have stood there wondering and asked: "But what have you done to us?" What forbearance they showed!

Often in the morning when I stood at my window and the busy day began to pour in upon me, I could even forget myself for a moment, I could look about me as if I were going to undertake something in which my being could still find delight, as once it did; but then I would rebuke myself, I would recollect myself like one who inadvertently utters a word of his mother tongue in some country where no one understands it—"Whither away, my heart?" I enjoined myself prudently, and obeyed.

"What is it for which man so immeasurably longs?" I often asked myself; "what is eternity doing in his breast? Eternity? Where is it? who has ever seen it? Man wants more than he is capable of! that seems to be the truth of it! Oh, you have experienced it often enough! And as it is, so it must be. This it is which bestows the sweet, rapturous sense of power: that our powers do not flow forth as they will—this it is, and nothing else, which creates our fair dreams of immortality and all the enticing, all the colossal phantoms that ravish men a thousand times over; this it is which creates his Elysium and his gods for man: that the line of his life does not run straight, that he does not speed to his goal like an arrow, that a power outside of him stops him in his flight.

"The heart's surging wave would not foam up so beautifully and become spirit, did not the ancient cliff of Fate stand silently opposing it.

"Yet, even so, the impulse dies in our breast, and with it our gods and their heaven.

"The fire leaps up in shapes of joy from the dark cradle

in which it slept, and its flame rises and falls, is gone and comes laughing back again, until that on which it fed is consumed; now it smokes and struggles and dies; and what remains is ashes.

"So it is with us. This is the heart of all that the wise teach us in forbidding and enticing mysteries.

"And you? why do you concern yourself? That now and again something rises up in you, and in one instant, like a dying man's mouth, your heart opens itself to you with such power and closes again—that is precisely the fatal symptom.

"Only be still and let things take their course! Stop devising! Stop childishly trying to add a cubit to your stature! —It is as if you wanted to create another sun and new creatures for it to nourish, to bring forth an earth and a moon."

So I dreamed on. Patiently, little by little, I took leave of everything.—O you who live in this age with me! seek not counsel of your doctors nor of your priests when your hearts wither away!

You have lost all faith in anything great; you are doomed, then, doomed to perish, then, unless that faith returns, like a comet from skies unknown.

Hyperion to Bellarmin

There is a forgetting of all existence, a hush of our being, in which we feel as if we had found all.

There is a hush, a forgetting of all existence, in which we feel as if we had lost all, a night of our soul, in which no glimmer of any star nor even the fox fire from a rotting log gives us light.

I had become quiet. No longer did anything drive me from bed at midnight. No longer did I singe myself in my own flame.

Now I looked straight before me, alone and impassive, nor did my eyes roam over the past and the future. No longer now did far and near jostle together in my mind. Unless men forced me to see them, I saw them not.

Once this century lay before my mind's eye like the eternally empty cask of the Danaïdes, and my soul poured itself out with prodigal love, to fill the void; now I saw no more void, now the ennui of life no longer oppressed me.

Never now did I say to the flower, "Thou art my sister," and to the springs, "We are of one race." Now, like an echo, I faithfully gave each thing its name.

Like a river past arid banks, where no willow leaf mirrors itself in the water, the world flowed past me untouched by beauty.

Hyperion to Bellarmin

Nothing can grow like man, nothing so utterly wither away. Time and again he compares his woe with the darkness of the abyss, his bliss with the ether, and how little does that tell of either!

But nothing is more beautiful than when, after a long death, it begins to dawn in him, and sorrow goes like a brother to meet distantly dawning joy.

Oh, it was with a heavenly anticipation that I now greeted the returning spring! Like the far music of the beloved's lyre in windless air when all is asleep, so spring's soft melodies sounded about my breast; as if wafting hither from Elysium, so I felt its coming, when the dead twigs stirred and a soft air brushed my cheek.

Lovely sky of Ionia! Never had I so looked to thee; but never had my heart been so like thee as then it was in its playful gaiety, its playful tenderness.—

Who does not long for the joys of love and for high deeds when spring returns to the eye of Heaven and the bosom of Earth?

I rose as from a sickbed, quietly and slowly, but my breast trembled so blissfully with secret hopes that I quite forgot to ask what this might mean.

More beautiful dreams now wrapped me when I slept, and when I woke they were in my heart, like the trace of a kiss on the cheek of the beloved. Oh! the morning light and I—we went to meet each other now like newly reconciled friends when they still hold back and yet already bear in their souls the coming, endless moment of their embrace.

Now once again my eye truly opened—not, to be sure, as once it did, armed and filled with strength from within me; it had become more entreating, it begged for life; but in my heart of hearts it was as if I could be again what once I had been, and better.

I looked at men again as if I, too, was to work among them and rejoice with them. I cordially and sincerely committed myself everywhere.

Heavens! what a sight for them to gloat over: the proud nonconformist brought low, become one of themselves! What a joke: the wild deer of the forest driven by hunger to come running into their barnyard!—

Ah! I looked for my Adamas, for my Alabanda, but neither of them appeared to me.

Finally, I even wrote to Smyrna, and, as I wrote, it was as if all the tenderness and all the strength of humanity were concentrated in that one moment; three times I wrote thus, but no answer came, I implored, threatened, evoked all our hours of love and courage, but no answer came from him of imperishable memory, from him whom I loved beyond life—"Alabanda!" I cried, "O my Alabanda! you have pronounced my death sentence. You kept me from falling, you were the last hope of my youth! Now I want nothing more, now it is sworn and sealed!"

We pity the dead as if they felt death, yet the dead have peace. But the pain, the pain that no pain equals, is the incessant feeling of utter annihilation when our life loses its meaning, when our heart bids itself "Down! into the depths! there is nothing left of you; you have planted no flower, built no hut, so that you might but say: I leave a trace behind me on earth." Yet, oh! the soul can always be so full of longing, even when it is so cast down!

I still sought for something, but I did not dare to raise my eyes in the presence of men. I went through hours when I feared the laughter of a child.

Yet for the most part I was perfectly quiet and patient, I even had a strangely superstitious belief in the healing power of many things: a dove that I bought, a row that I took, a valley that the mountains hid from me—from these I could hope for comfort.

Enough! enough! Had I grown up with Themistocles, had I lived among the Scipios, my soul would never have come to know itself in this light.

Hyperion to Bellarmin

At times some energy would even yet waken in my spirit. But only for destruction!

What is man?—so I might begin. How does it happen that the world contains such a thing, which ferments like a chaos or moulders like a rotten tree, and never grows to ripeness? How can Nature tolerate this sour grape among her sweet clusters?

To the plants he says: I, too, was once like ye! and to the pure stars: I shall become like ye in another world! —meanwhile he falls to pieces and keeps practicing his arts on himself, as if, once it had come apart, he could put a living thing together again like a piece of masonry; but it does not disconcert him if nothing is the better for all his efforts; yet what he does will always be but artifice.

Oh, you wretches who feel all this, who, even as I, cannot allow yourselves to speak of man's being here for a purpose, who, even as I, are so utterly in the clutch of the Nothing that governs us, so profoundly aware that we are born for nothing, that we love a nothing, believe in nothing, work ourselves to death for nothing only that little by little we may pass over into nothing—how can I help it if your knees fail you when you think of it in earnest? Many a time have I, too, sunk into these bottom-

less thoughts, and cried out: Why do you lay the axe to
my root, pitiless spirit?—and still I am here.

Oh, once, my brothers in darkness, it was otherwise.
Then all was so fair above us, all so fair and joyous before us; our hearts, too, overflowed before the distant,
blessed phantoms, our spirits, too, strove upward bold
and exulting and broke the barriers—and, when they
looked about, alas! there was only endless emptiness.

Oh, I can fall to my knees and wring my hands and
pray—but to whom?—for other thoughts. But I cannot
overcome it, the screaming truth. Have I not twice convinced myself? When I look at life, what is last of all?
Nothing. When I arise in spirit, what is highest of all?
Nothing.

But be still, my heart! This is your last strength that
you are wasting! Your last strength? and you—you would
storm heaven? then where are your hundred arms, Titan,
where your Pelion and Ossa, your stairway to the city of
the Father of the Gods, that you may climb it and throw
down the God and his divine banquet and the summit of
Olympus, and preach to mortals: Remain below, children
of the moment! seek not to reach these heights, for there
is nothing here above.

You may well leave off watching what governs others,
my heart. Your new knowledge is meant for you. Sure
enough, before you and above you there is emptiness and
desolation, because there is emptiness and desolation within you.

To be sure, if you other men are richer than I am,
you might just help a little.

If your garden is so full of flowers, why does not their
breath rejoice me too?—If you are so filled with divinity,
give me to drink of it. At feasts no one starves, not even
the poorest. But only *one* holds his feast among you; and
that is Death.

Sorrow and Fear and Darkness are your lords. They
part you, they drive you together with blows. You call
hunger love, and where you see nothing more, there dwell
your gods. Gods? and love?

Oh, the poets are right, there is nothing so little and

of so little account that man could not know rapture by it.

So I thought. How all this came to be in me, I still do not understand.

BOOK TWO

Hyperion to Bellarmin

I now live on Ajax's island, dear Salamis.

I love all of this Greece. It wears the color of my heart. Wherever you look, a joy lies buried.

And yet there is so much that is delightful, so much that is great, about one.

On the promontory I have built a hut of mastic branches, and planted moss and trees about it, and thyme and every kind of shrub.

There I spend my favorite hours, there I sit evening after long evening, gazing across at Attica, until finally my heart beats too strongly; then I gather up my gear, go down to the bay, and catch fish.

Or, up on my hill, I read of the ancient, magnificent sea fight that once blazed up at Salamis in wild but skillfully controlled confusion; I rejoice in the mind that could guide and master the fierce chaos of friends and foes as a rider does his horse, and I feel deeply ashamed of my own career as a soldier.

Or I gaze out over the sea and reflect upon my life, its heights and its depths, its bliss and its sorrow, and often my past comes back to me like the sound of a lyre on which the master runs through every tone, blending discord and harmony in obedience to a hidden plan.

Today up here it is trebly beautiful. Two gracious days of rain have cooled the air and the weary earth.

The ground has turned greener, the fields are more

open. The golden wheat stands endless, mingled with
cheery cornflowers, and a thousand hopeful crowns rise
from the depth of the grove. Every faintest or boldest line
of the distance is conveyed through space; one behind
the other, the mountains rise unbroken to the sun, like
a flight of steps. The whole sky is pure. The white light
is but breathed over the ether, and like a little silver cloud
the shy moon goes floating across the bright day.

Hyperion to Bellarmin

It is long since I have been as now I am.

As Jupiter's eagle listens for the song of the Muses, so
I listen for the marvelous, unending euphony in me. Undisturbed in mind and soul, strong and joyous and smilingly serious, I play with Fate and the Three Sisters, the
holy Parcae. Full of divine youth, my whole being rejoices over itself, over all things. Like the starry sky, I
am calm yet moved.

I have waited long for such a holiday time, that I
might write to you once again. Now I am strong enough;
now let me tell on.

In the midst of my dark days, a friend from Calaurea
invited me over to visit him. I must come to his mountains, he insisted; life there was freer than anywhere else,
and there, too, amid the pinewoods and the enchanting
streams, there were lemon groves and palms and lovely
herbage and myrtles and the sacred grape. He had planted
a garden high in the mountains and built a house; close-
set trees shaded it from behind, and cooling airs played
softly about it in the burning days of summer; from it,
like a bird from the top of a cedar, one looked down
into the low country, over the villages and green hills
and peaceful homes of the island, lying like children about
the glorious mountain and drawing their nourishment from
its foaming brooks.

That roused me a little, even then. It was on a bright,
blue April day that I sailed over. The sea was unusually

beautiful and pure, the air as light as in higher regions. In the gliding bark we left the earth behind, as one leaves a delicious dish when the sacred wine is handed round.

My dark moods strove in vain against the influence of sea and air. I surrendered myself, cared neither about myself nor others, sought for nothing, thought of nothing, let the boat rock me half asleep, and imagined that I was lying in Charon's bark. Oh, it is sweet so to drink from the cup of oblivion.

My cheerful skipper wanted to strike up a conversation with me, but I was very monosyllabic. He kept pointing to islands right and left, but I did not look long, and the next minute I was back in my own sweet dreams.

Finally when he pointed out quiet peaks in the distance and said that we should soon reach Calaurea, I became more attentive, and my whole being opened to the marvelous power that, sweet and still and inexplicable, suddenly played upon me. Wide-eyed, astonished and happy, I gazed out into the secrets of the distance, my heart trembled a little, my hand escaped me and hastened to grasp my skipper affectionately.—"What!" I cried, "is that Calaurea?" And as he turned to look at me in surprise, I was myself at a loss what to make of myself. I greeted my friend with the greatest fondness. My whole being was full of sweet unrest.

That very afternoon I set out to explore part of the island. The woods and secret valleys attracted me indescribably, and the charming day lured everything out.

It was so plain to see that all living things crave more than daily bread, that the bird, too, has its festal banquet, and the beast.

It was enchanting to look on! As when a mother cajolingly asks where her dearest pet has got to, and all her children come rushing to her lap and even the littlest reaches out its arms from the cradle, so every life flew and leaped and struggled out into the divine air, and beetles and swallows and doves and storks circled together in joyous confusion in its depths and heights, and the steps of all that were earthbound became flight, the horse charged over the furrows and the roebuck over the hedges, the fish came up from the bottom of the sea and leaped over the surface. Air, the mother, affected the hearts of all, uplifted all and drew them to her.

And men came out of their doors, and wonderfully did they feel the heady air as it lightly moved the fine hairs over their brows, as it cooled the sun's ray, and happily they loosed their garments to receive it upon their breasts, and breathed more sweetly, felt more gently touched by the light, cool, soothing sea in which they lived and moved and had their being.

O Sister of the spirit that lives in us and rules us with fiery power, holy Air! how beautiful it is that, no matter where I wander, thou goest with me, all-present, immortal one!

It was with the children that the high element played most beautifully.

One hummed happily to himself, a little rhythmless song rose from another's lips, a shout of joy from another's open throat; one stretched, one leaped high; another strolled about, lost to the world.

And all this was the language of a single sense of well-being, all was one answer to the caresses of the ravishing breezes.

I was filled with indescribable longing and peace. A power without me ruled me. Kindly Spirit, I said to myself, whither callest thou me? to Elysium, or whither?

I went up through a wood, following purling waters as, here, they trickled down a cliff, there glided innocently over pebbles; and little by little the valley grew narrower and became an arcade, and the light of high noon played solitary in the still darkness—

Here—would that I could speak, my Bellarmin! would that I could write to you, calmly.

Speak? Oh, I am a novice in joy, I want to speak!

Does not silence dwell in the Land of the Blessed? Above the stars the heart forgets its needs and its language.

I have guarded it sacredly! I have carried it within me like a palladium—the divine that appeared to me! and if henceforth Fate lays hold of me and casts me from abyss to abyss and drowns all powers in me and all thoughts: yet shall this unique revelation outlive myself

in me and shine in me and rule me, in eternal, indestructible brightness!—

So didst thou lie poured out, sweet life, so didst thou
look up, and arise, and stand there before me in delicate
completeness, divinely calm, and with thy heavenly face
filled with the serene ecstasy in which I disturbed thee!

Oh, he who has looked into the stillness of those eyes,
he for whom those sweet lips have opened—of what else
can he speak?

Peace of beauty! divine peace! he whose raging life,
whose doubting spirit, has once been soothed by thee—
what can aught else avail him?

I cannot speak of her; but there are hours when the
best and most beautiful appears as in clouds, and the
heaven of crowning perfection opens before the surmise
of love; in such a moment, Bellarmin, think of her being,
in such a moment go down on your knees with me and
think of my bliss! but forget not that I had what you
only surmise, that I saw with these eyes what appears to
you only as in clouds.

That men will sometimes say they are happy! Oh, believe me, ye who speak thus, ye have had no faintest
inkling of what happiness is! Not the shadow of its shadow
has yet appeared to you! O blindmen, depart, and speak
not of the blue ether!

That one can become as children are, that still the
golden age of innocence returns, the time of peace and
freedom; that one happiness, one place of rest remains
upon earth!

Does not man grow old and shrivelled, is he not like a
fallen leaf that finds not its branch again and is driven
hither and yon by the winds, until the sand buries it?

And yet his spring returns!

Weep not, when the best fades, it will soon revive! Mourn
not, when the melody of your hearts falls silent, soon
will a hand be found to tune it again!

How was it with me, then? Was I not like a shattered
lyre? I sounded a little still, but they were tones of death.
I had sung a mournful swan song for myself! Gladly
would I have woven myself a funeral wreath, but I had
only winter flowers.

And where, then, was it now—the deathly silence, the darkness and emptiness of my life? all that paltry mortality?

True enough, life is wretched and lonely. We live here below like the diamond in the mine. In vain we ask where we went astray, that we may find the way upward again.

We are like fire that sleeps in the dry branch or in the coal; and ever we struggle and seek for an end to our cramped confinement. But they come, they make up for aeons of struggle, the moments when we are set free, when the divine shatters the prison, when the flame bursts from the wood and wings up over the ashes, ah! when it is with us as if, its sorrows and its servitude forgotten, the unshackled spirit were returning in triumph to the halls of the Sun.

Hyperion to Bellarmin

Once I was happy, Bellarmin! Am I not so still? Should I not be happy even if the sacred moment when first I saw her had been the last?

I have seen it once, the one thing that my soul sought; and the perfection that we put somewhere far away above the stars, that we put off until the end of time— I have felt it in its living presence. There it was, all that is highest! in this circle of human nature and of things, it was there!

I no longer ask where it may be; it was in the world, it can return into it, it is in the world now, only more hiddenly. I no longer ask what it is; I have seen it, have known it.

O ye who seek the highest and the best, whether in the depths of knowledge, in the turmoil of action, in the darkness of the past, in the labyrinth of the future, in graves or above the stars! do ye know its name? the name of that which is one and is all?

Its name is Beauty.

Did ye know what ye sought? I know it not yet, but I surmise it as from afar, the new kingdom of the new divinity, and I hasten toward it and seize upon others and take them with me, as the river the rivers to the ocean.

And you, you showed me the way! With you I began. They are not worth speech, the days when yet I knew you not—

O Diotima, Diotima, divine being!

Hyperion to Bellarmin

Let us forget that time exists and cease to reckon the days of our lives!

What are centuries compared to the moment when two beings thus divine and approach each other?

I still see the evening when Notara took me to visit her for the first time.

She lived only a few hundred paces from us, at the foot of the mountain.

Her mother was a thoughtful, tender being, her brother a simple, happy lad, and both of them, in all that they did, gladly acknowledged that Diotima was the queen of the household.

Ah, everything was blessed and beautified by her presence. Wherever I looked, whatever I touched, the rug before her chair, her cushion, her little table—they were all mysteriously allied to her. And, oh, the first time she addressed me by my name, that she came so close to me that her innocent breath touched my listening being!—

We spoke to each other very little. Speech abashes. Music alone would serve: to become all music and unite with each other in one celestial melody!

And of what were we to speak? We saw nothing but each other. Of that we did not dare to speak.

In the end we spoke of the life of the Earth.

Never has a hymn at once so ardent and so childlike been sung to her.

It did us good to bestrew our kindly Mother's lap with what overbrimmed our hearts. We felt relieved, as the trees do when the summer wind shakes their fruitful branches and pours their sweet apples over the grass.

We called Earth one of the flowers of Heaven, and Heaven the infinite garden of life. As roses gladden one another with golden dust, we said, even so does the heroic sunlight gladden Earth with its rays; she is a glorious living being, we said, alike divine when raging fire or sweet clear water pours from her heart; ever happy, whether she be nourished by dewdrops, or by thunder-clouds that she prepares for her delight with the sky's aid; she is the ever more faithfully loving mate of the Sun God, perhaps in the beginning more intimately united with him but then divided from him by some all-powerful Fate, so that now she seeks him, approaches him, draws away, and, between joy and sorrow, ripens to the highest beauty.

So we spoke. I give you the gist, the essence of it. But what is that without the life?

Twilight fell; it was time to go. "Good night, ye angel eyes!" I thought in my heart. "Appear to me soon again, thou beautiful, divine spirit, with thy peace and thine abundance!"

Hyperion to Bellarmin

Some days later they came up to visit us. We walked about the garden together. Diotima and I found ourselves ahead of the others, absorbed; tears of ecstasy often rose to my eyes for the holiness that walked so unpretentiously beside me.

Now we were standing close to the summit's rim, gazing out into the endless East.

Diotima's eyes opened wide; and softly, as a bud unfolds, that sweet face unfolded under the airs of heaven, became pure speech and soul, and, as if beginning to rise among the clouds, her whole figure stood drawn gracefully up in gentle majesty, her feet scarcely touching the ground.

Oh, could I have caught her under the arms, as the

eagle grasps his Ganymede, and flown away with her over the sea and the islands!

Now she stepped yet farther forward, and gazed down the precipitous rock wall. She found a pleasure in gauging the terrifying depths and losing herself in the night of the woods that raised their lustrous crowns from among fallen rocks and foaming, storm-swollen streams.

The balustrade against which she was leaning was rather low. So I dared to hold the charming creature a moment, while thus she leaned forward. Ah! hot, trembling rapture coursed through my being, my every sense reeled and was confounded, my hands burned like coals, when I touched her.

And then the profound joy of standing so familiarly beside her, and my tender, childish fear lest she might fall, and my delight in the glorious maiden's enthusiasm!

What is all that men have done and thought over thousands of years, compared with one moment of love? But in all Nature, too, it is what is nearest to perfection, what is most divinely beautiful! Thither all stairs lead from the threshold of life. Thence we come, thither we go.

Hyperion to Bellarmin

The one thing that I should forget is her singing, only that music from the soul should never return into my unending dreams.

We do not know the proudly sailing swan when it sits asleep on the bank.

Only when she sang could one know the sweet, silent one who was so reluctant to speak.

Only then did that divinely uncomplaisant maiden appear in her majesty and her charm; then, then did her tender, blossoming lips breathe now cajolery and flattery, now the sternness of a divine decree. And what a quickened heart there was in that divine voice, how all pride and all humility, all the joy and sorrow of life appeared beautified in the nobility of those tones!

As the swallow catches bees in flight, so she ever seized us all.

It was not delight, not wonder that arose among us, it was the peace of heaven.

A thousand times have I said it to her and to myself: the most beautiful is also the most sacred. And such was everything in her. Like her singing, even so was her life.

Hyperion to Bellarmin

Her heart was at home among flowers, as if itself were a flower.

She named them all by their names, or out of her love for them gave them new and more beautiful ones, she knew exactly which was the happiest season for each of them.

Like a sister when a dear brother or sister comes running to her from every corner, and each would be greeted first, so was her quiet being busy with hand and eye, blissfully distracted, when we walked to the meadows or the woods.

And all this was so utterly unaffected and uncalculated in her, it was so much a part of her own growth.

It is eternally true, it is visible everywhere: the more innocent, the more beautiful a soul is, the more familiarly will it live with those other happy beings to which men deny souls.

Hyperion to Bellarmin

A thousand times in the joy of my heart have I laughed at people who imagine that a noble spirit cannot possibly know how to cook a vegetable. At the proper time Diotima could speak stoutly of the hearth; and surely there is nothing nobler than a noble maiden who tends the all-beneficent flame and, like Nature herself, prepares the food that gladdens the heart.

Hyperion to Bellarmin

What is all the artful knowledge in the world, what is all the proud autonomy of human thought, compared with the unstudied music of this spirit, which knew not what it knew or what it was?

Who would not rather choose the full, fresh grape-cluster as it sprang from the root, than the picked and dried grapes that the merchant presses into the box and sends out into the world? What is the wisdom of a book compared with the wisdom of an angel?

She always seemed to say so little, and said so much.

One late twilight I was seeing her home; dewy mists were gliding over the field, the blessed stars looked down through the twigs like watchful Geniuses.

Rarely was a "How beautiful!" heard from her lips, even though her reverent heart left no whispering leaf, no purling brook unheard and unheeded.

But this time she said it aloud to me: "How beautiful!"

"Perhaps it is so to please us!" I said casually, as children say something, neither in jest nor in earnest.

"I can imagine that it is as you say," she answered; "I like best to think of the world as of life in a household of which each member, without exactly thinking about it, adapts himself to all the others, in which all live pleasing and rejoicing one another simply because that is what springs from their hearts."

"A happy and noble truth!" I cried.

She was silent for a while.

"Then we, too, are children in such a household," I finally resumed; "we are, and shall be."

"Shall ever be," she answered.

"Shall we?" I asked.

"In this," she continued, "I trust Nature, as daily I trust her."

Oh, how I wished that I could have been Diotima as she said this! But you do not know what she said, my Bellarmin! You neither saw it nor heard it.

"You are right," I cried. "Eternal Beauty, the eternal Beauty that is Nature, suffers no loss as she suffers no addition. Her ornaments are different tomorrow from what they were today; but she cannot dispense with what is best in us, with us, with us ourselves, and least of all with you. We believe that we are eternal because our souls feel the beauty of Nature. She will be a mere patchwork, she will be neither divine nor complete, if ever you are lacking to her. She does not deserve your heart if she must blush before your hopes."

Hyperion to Bellarmin

Such freedom from wants, such divine content I have never found before.

As the ocean swell about the shores of happy isles, so the peace of the heavenly maiden flowed about my restless heart.

I had nothing to give her except a mind full of wild contradictions, full of bleeding memories, I had nothing to give her except my boundless love with its thousand cares, its thousand furious hopes; but she stood before me in changeless beauty, effortless, in smiling perfection; and all the visions, all the dreams of mortality, ah! all that the Genius presages of higher regions in golden morning hours—it was all fulfilled in that one calm soul.

Men say that the battle will die away beyond the stars; only after our lees have sunk, they promise us, will fermenting life be changed into the noble vintage of joy; men look no more on this earth for the heart-whole rest of the blessed. I know otherwise. I have taken the shorter way. I stood before her, and heard and saw the peace of Heaven; and in the very midst of this sighing chaos, Urania appeared to me.

How often have I stilled my grieving before that image!

how often have arrogant life and the striving mind been
pacified when, sunk in blessed contemplation, I looked
into her heart, as one looks into a spring when it trembles
silently under the touch of the sky that trickles down on
it in drops of silver!

She was my Lethe, her soul my sacred Lethe, from
which I drank forgetfulness of existence, so that I stood
before her like an immortal and joyously rebuked myself
and, as if after oppressive dreams, could not but smile
at all the chains that had hung heavy on me.

Oh, I could have become a happy man, an admirable
man with her!

With her! But that went wrong; and now I wander
about in what is before me and in me, and on beyond,
and know not what to make of myself and other things.

My soul is like a fish cast up out of its element on the
sand of the beach, and it writhes and flings itself about
until it dries up in the heat of the day.

Ah! were there but something left in the world for me
to do! were there work for me, a war for me—that would
refresh me!

Boys torn from their mother's breasts and cast out into
the wilderness were once, so they say, suckled by a she-
wolf.

My heart is not so fortunate.

Hyperion to Bellarmin

I can speak of her only fragmentarily—a word here, a
word there. I have to forget what she is in her completeness if I am to speak of her at all. I have to trick myself
into believing that she lived long, long ago, that I know
only a little about her from hearsay, if her living image
is not so to overwhelm me that I perish in rapture and
woe, if I am not to die of delight in her and die of
grief for her.

Hyperion to Bellarmin

It is in vain; I cannot hide it from myself. Wherever I flee with my thoughts, be it up to the heavens or into the abyss, to the beginning and to the end of Time, even if I turn to that which was my last refuge, which consumed every other grief in me, which burned up every other joy and woe of life for me in the flame in which it revealed itself, even if I cast myself into the arms of that glorious, secret Spirit of the World, plunge into its depths as into the boundless ocean—there, even there the sweet terror finds me, the sweet, brain-turning, mortal terror: that Diotima's grave is near me.

Do you hear? do you hear? Diotima's grave!

Yet my heart had grown so quiet, and my love was buried with the dead one whom I loved.

You know, my Bellarmin, that for a long time I did not write to you of her, and when I wrote, I wrote to you calmly, or so I think?

So what is it now?

I go down to the shore and look across to Calaurea, where she rests—it is that.

Oh, may no one lend me his boat, may no one have pity on me and offer me his oars and take me across to her!

May the kindly sea not remain calm, that I may not cut myself a piece of wood and swim across to her.

But let the sea rage and I will fling myself into it and ask its waves to cast me on Diotima's shore!—

Dear brother! I comfort my heart with all sorts of imaginings, I pour myself many a sleeping potion; and surely it would be nobler to free oneself forever than to make shift with palliatives; but who does not fare likewise? So I am content to have it so.

Content! that would be a fine thing! that would be the help that is needed where no god can help.

Softly, now! I have done what I could! I call on Fate to give me back my soul.

Hyperion to Bellarmin

Was she not mine, ye Fatal Sisters, was she not mine? I summon the pure springs to witness, and the innocent trees that saw and heard us, and the light of day and the ether! was she not mine? at one with me in all the various music of life?

Where is the being that knew her as mine did? In what mirror, as in me, were all the rays of that light concentrated? was she not joyously terrified by her own splendor when first she became conscious of it in my joy? Ah! where is the heart that filled her and was filled by her like mine? that existed only, only to embrace hers, as the eyelash exists for the eye?

We were but one flower; and our souls lived in each other, like the flower when it loves and hides its tender joys in its closed cup.

And yet, and yet—was she not torn from me like a crown usurped, and laid in the dust?

Hyperion to Bellarmin

Before either of us knew it, we belonged to each other. When, with all the homage of my heart, blissfully conquered, I stood before her, saying nothing, and all my life offered itself up in the gaze of my eyes that saw only her, embraced only her, and she in turn looked at me in tender uncertainty, not knowing where my thoughts had come to rest; when often, absorbed in delight and beauty, I watched her at some charming task, and about her slightest movement, as the bee about the swaying twig, my soul darted and flew, and when then she turned to me in calm thought, and, startled by my joy, had to hide my joy from herself, and sought for peace in her dear task again, and found it—

When, in her miraculous omniscience, she caught every harmony, every dissonance in the depths of my being and revealed them to me before I was even aware of them, when she saw every shadow of a cloud on my brow, every shadow of melancholy, of pride, on my lips, every spark in my eyes, when she listened for the ebb and flow of my heart, and sadly foreboded troubled hours as my spirit spent itself too intemperately and prodigally in exuberant speeches, when the dear being showed me every change in my face more faithfully than a mirror, and often in loving concern reproved me for my unstable being and scolded me as one scolds a cherished child—

Ah! when once, innocent Diotima, you counted on your fingers the steps that led down from our mountain to your house, when you showed me your walks, the places where you had been wont to sit, and told me how the hours had passed for you then, and said at last that now it seemed to you as if I had always been there too—

Had we not then long since belonged to each other?

Hyperion to Bellarmin

I dig my heart a grave, that it may rest; I spin a cocoon about myself, because it is winter everywhere; I wrap myself against the storm in blissful memories.

One day we were sitting in Diotima's garden under blossoming almond trees, with Notara (such was the name of the friend in whose house I was living) and a few others who, like ourselves, were among the nonconformists in Calaurea, talking, among other things, about friendship.

I had scarcely joined in the conversation; for some time I had avoided saying much about things that lie closest to the heart, so taciturn had my Diotima made me.—

"When Harmodius and Aristogiton were alive," someone cried at last, "friendship still existed in the world."
That pleased me too much for me to remain silent.

"We should twine you a wreath in reward for those
words!" I cried. "But have you really any notion, any
image, of the friendship between Aristogiton and Harmodius? Forgive me! But, by the Ether! one must *be*
Aristogiton to have a sense of how Aristogiton loved, and
surely he must not fear lightning who would be loved
with Harmodius' love, for I am mistaken in everything
if the terrible youth did not love with all the sternness
of Minos. Few have come off successfully in such a test,
and it is no easier to be the friend of a demigod than,
like Tantalus, to sit at the table of the gods. But by the
same token there is nothing more glorious on earth than
when such a proud pair as they are so sovereign over each
other.

"This is my hope, too, my longing and my joy in solitary hours, that such noble tones, yes, and nobler, must
yet sound again in the symphony of the world's course.
Love brought to birth millenniums filled with living men;
friendship will give birth to them again. Once upon a
time the peoples set forth from the harmony of childhood;
the harmony of spirits will be the beginning of another
history of man. Men began and grew from the happiness
of the plant, grew until they ripened; from that time on
they have been in ceaseless ferment, inwardly and outwardly, until now mankind lies there like a Chaos, utterly
disintegrated, so that all who can still feel and see are
dizzied; but Beauty forsakes the life of men, flees upward
into Spirit; the Ideal becomes what Nature was, and even
though the tree is dried out and weatherworn below, a
fresh crown has still sprung from it and flourishes green
in the sunlight as the trunk did once in its days of youth;
the Ideal is what Nature was. By this, by this Ideal, this
rejuvenated divinity, the few recognize one another and
are one, for one thing is in them; and from them, from
them, the world's second age begins—I have said enough
to make it clear what I think."

You should have seen Diotima then, springing up and

giving me both her hands and crying: "I have understood it, beloved, much as it means, understood it all.

"Love bore the world, friendship will bear it again.

"Therefore, O ye of the future, ye new Dioscuri, therefore linger a little when ye pass by the place where Hyperion sleeps, linger in sympathy over the forgotten man's ashes, and say: He would be like one of us, were he here now."

This I heard, my Bellarmin, this was granted to me; and shall I not willingly go to my death?

Yes, yes! I have already had my reward, I have lived. A god could bear more joy, but not I.

Hyperion to Bellarmin

Do you ask how it was with me at that time? As with one who has lost all to gain all.

To be sure, I often came from Diotima's trees like one intoxicated with victory, often I had to hurry away from her lest I betray any of my thoughts; so did joy rage in me, and my pride and my boundless rapture in believing that Diotima loved me.

Then I sought out the highest mountains and their air, and like the eagle whose bleeding pinion has healed, my spirit moved in freedom, spread itself over the visible world as if the world belonged to it; strange to tell, I often felt as if the things of earth were purified and fused together like gold in my fire, and something divine arose from them and me, so did joy rage in me; and oh! how I picked up the children and clasped them to my throbbing heart! how I greeted the plants and the trees! I could have wished that I possessed a spell to gather all the shy deer and the wild birds of the forest like a happy family about my prodigal hands—in such blissful folly did I love all things.

But not for long—and then all this was extinguished in me like a light, and speechless and mournful as a shade

I sat and sought for the life that had vanished. I felt no wish to complain, no wish to console myself. I cast away hope as a lame man casts away his broken crutch; I was ashamed to weep; I was ashamed to exist. Yet in the end my pride burst out in tears, and the pain that I would have disowned became dear to me, and I took it to my breast like a child.

"No," cried my heart, "no, my Diotima! it does not hurt. Preserve your peace, and let me go my way. Let it not disturb your quietude, pure star! that there is ferment and murk below you.

"Oh, let not your rose fade, blessed springtime of the gods! Let not your beauty age in the trials of earth. This, this is my joy, sweet life! that you bear carefree Heaven within you. You are not made to become a pauper, no, no! you shall not see yourself destitute of love."

And when again I went down to her—I should have liked to ask the breeze and try to divine from the drift of the clouds how it would be with me in an hour! And how happy I was when some friendly face met me on the way and called "A lovely day!" to me not too mechanically.

When a little girl came out of the woods and held out a bunch of strawberries for me to buy, but with a look as if she wanted to give them to me; or when a farmer, sitting in his cherry tree picking as I passed, called down to me from among the branches and asked if I would not like a handful to taste—those were good omens to my superstitious heart!

If one of Diotima's windows stood wide open toward the road by which I came down, what good that did me!

Perhaps she had been looking out of it not long before.

And now I stood before her, breathless and wavering, and pressed my crossed arms against my heart that I might not feel its trembling, and as the swimmer struggles out from the clutching tide, so my spirit strove and struggled not to drown in endless love.

"What shall we talk about, I wonder?" I would cry. "It is often difficult, finding a subject from which one's thoughts will not stray."

"Are they off into the air again?" my Diotima answered. "You must fasten lead to their wings, or I will tie a string to them as a boy does to a kite, so that we shall not lose them."

The dear girl was trying to help us both out by jesting, but it was little use.

"Yes, yes!" I cried, "whatever you say, whatever you think best—shall I read aloud? Your lute is probably still in tune from yesterday and I really have nothing to read—"

"You have more than once promised," she said, "to tell me of your life before we came to know each other—will you not do it now?"

"True," I said. My heart plunged into it eagerly, and I told her, as I have told you, of Adamas and my lonely days in Smyrna, of Alabanda and how I was parted from him, and of the strange sickness that afflicted my being before I came over to Calaurea—"Now you know all," I told her calmly when I had ended, "now you will find me less objectionable; now you will say," I added with a smile, " 'Do not laugh at this Vulcan if he limps, for the gods have twice flung him down from heaven to earth.' "

"Be still," she cried in a choked voice, and hid her tears in her handkerchief, "oh, be still, and do not mock your destiny, your heart! for I understand them, and better than you do.

"Dear—dear Hyperion. You are indeed hard to help.

"Do you not know," she continued, raising her voice, "do you not know what you are starving for, the one thing that you lack, what you are seeking as Alpheus his Arethusa, what you mourn for in all your sorrow? It did not vanish years ago, it is impossible to say exactly when it was there, when it went; but it was, it is—it is in you! It is a better age, that is what you seek, a more beautiful world. It was that world alone that you embraced in your friends, with them you were in that world.

"It rose for you in Adamas; with him it set for you. In Alabanda its light appeared to you for the second time, but more fiercely and searingly, and so it was like midnight about your soul when you found him gone.

"Now do you see, too, why the least doubt of Alabanda could not but become despair in you? why you repudiated him, only because he was not quite a god?

"It was no man that you wanted, believe me, you wanted a world. The loss of all golden centuries, crowded together, as you felt them, in one happy moment, the spirit of all spirits of a better time, the strength of all the strength of heroes—you wanted one man to take their place for you! —Do you not see now how poor, how rich, you are? why you must be so proud and so downcast? why joy and sorrow visit you in such dreadful alternation?

"It is because you have everything and nothing, because the phantom of the golden days that must come belongs to you and yet is not here, because you are a dweller in the regions of Justice and Beauty, are a god among gods in the beautiful dreams that steal upon you by day, and when you awaken you find yourself standing on the soil of modern Greece.

"Twice, did you say? Oh, in a single day you are flung from heaven to earth a hundred times. Shall I say it? I fear for you, you can ill endure the destiny of this age. You will yet attempt many things, you will—

"Oh, God! and your last refuge will be a grave!"

"No, Diotima," I cried, "no! by Heaven, no! So long as one melody still sounds for me, I fear not the deathly stillness of the wilderness under the stars; so long as the sun shines, and Diotima, there is no night for me.

"Let the death bell toll for every virtue! yet I hear you, you, the song of your heart, O you whom I love! and find immortal life, while all things else sputter out, fade away."

"Hyperion," she cried, "what are you saying?"

"I say what I must. I can no longer, no longer hide all my bliss and fear and anxiety—Diotima!—Yes, you know it, must know it, you have long since seen that I perish if you do not reach out your hand to me."

She was astonished, bewildered.

"And is it I," she cried, "is it I in whom Hyperion would seek support? yes, I wish—now for the first time I wish—that I were more than a mortal maiden. But I am to you what I can be."

"Oh, then you are all to me!" I cried.

"All? wicked hypocrite! what, then, of humanity, your last and only love?"

"Humanity?" I said; "let humanity make Diotima its watchword and paint your picture on its banner and say: 'Today shall the divine have victory!' Angel from heaven! what a day that would be!"

"Go," she cried, "go, and show heaven your transfiguration! It must not be so close to me.

"You *will* go, will you not, dear Hyperion?"

I obeyed. Who in my place would not have obeyed? I went. Never before had I gone from her thus, O Bellarmin! it was joy, serenity of life, divine peace, heavenly, wondrous, unfathomable joy!

Words avail not here, and he who would seek her like has never known her. The one thing that could express such a joy was Diotima's own singing when it floated between height and depth, in the golden mean.

O ye meadows on the banks of Lethe! ye sunset paths to the woods of Elysium! ye lilies by the valley's streams! ye garlands of roses about the hill! I believe in you in this gracious hour and say to my heart: There you will find her again, and all the joy that you lost.

Hyperion to Bellarmin

I will tell you more and yet more of my happiness.

I will try the temper of my heart on the joys of the past until it is like steel, I will exercise myself upon them until I am invincible.

Ha! do they not often fall upon my soul like a sword-stroke? but I play with the sword until I am used to it, I hold my hand in the fire until I can bear it as if it were water.

I will not faint; yes! I will be strong! I will hide nothing from myself, will conjure up the bliss of all blisses from the grave.

It is incredible that a man should fear the most beautiful; yet it is so.

Oh, have I not fled a hundred times from these moments, this mortal ecstasy of my memories, turned away my eyes as a child does from lightning? Yet in the luxuriant garden of the world there grows nothing lovelier than my joys, neither in heaven nor on earth does anything nobler flourish than my joys.

But only to you, my Bellarmin, only to a pure, free soul like yours, do I tell it. I will not be as lavish as the sun with its rays; I will not cast my pearls before the unknowing multitude.

After that last conversation in which our souls met, I knew myself less every day. I felt that there was a holy secret between me and Diotima.

I wondered, I dreamed. As if a blessed spirit had appeared to me at midnight and chosen me to be his companion—such was the state of my soul.

Oh, it is a strange mixture of bliss and melancholy when it becomes apparent to us that we are forever outside of ordinary existence.

After that, I never managed to see Diotima alone. There was always some third person to intrude on us, separate us, and the world lay between her and me like an unbounded emptiness. Six days of mortal dread passed in this way, during which I had no knowledge of Diotima. It was as if the others about us paralyzed my senses, as if they killed my entire outward life, so that there was no way by which my imprisoned soul could reach her.

If I tried to find her with my eyes, night fell around me; if I tried to approach her with a word, it stuck in my throat.

Ah! my heart was often torn to pieces by my sacred, ineffable longing, my love often raged in me as powerfully as an imprisoned Titan. Never before had my spirit strained so fervently, so implacably, against the chains that Fate wrought for it, against the iron, inexorable law that kept it separate, that would not let it be one soul with its adorable other half.

The star-bright night had now become my element. Then, when all was still, as in the depths of the earth where gold multiplies in secret, then the more beautiful life of my love began.

Then my heart indulged its poetic right. It told me how Hyperion's spirit had played with his dear Diotima in the

Elysium of the unborn before it came down to earth, in divine childhood innocence, beside the music of the fountain and under branches that were like earthly branches when we see them gleam beautified from a golden stream.

And, like the past, the gates of the future opened within me.

We flew, Diotima and I, we wandered from one springtime of the world to another, though all the Sun's wide realm and beyond, to the other isles of heaven, to the golden shores of Sirius and Arcturus' vale of spirits—

Oh, how it crowns our longing to drink the joy of the world from one cup with the beloved!

Intoxicated by the blissful lullaby that I sang to myself, I fell asleep amid those glorious phantoms.

But when the life of the earth was kindled again by the rays of morning, I looked up and sought for the dreams of the night. Like the lovely stars, they had vanished, and only my ecstasy of grief bore witness to them in my soul.

I mourned; but I believe that there is such mourning among the blessed, too. It was the messenger of joy, this grief, it was the gray dawn in which the countless roses of crimson morning bud.—

The burning summer day had now driven all things to seek refuge in the deepest shade. In Diotima's house, too, all was now still and empty, and the envious curtains stood in my way at every window.

I lived in thoughts of her. Where are you, I thought, where shall my lonely spirit find you, sweet maiden? Do you stare aimlessly and muse? Have you laid your work aside to sit with elbow on knee and your head on your little hand, giving yourself to lovely thoughts?

Let nothing disturb her peace if my quiet one is refreshing her heart with sweet fancies, let nothing touch this cluster of grapes and wring the quickening juice from its delicate berries.

So I dreamed. But while my thoughts went looking for her inside the walls of the house, my feet sought her elsewhere, and before I knew it I was walking under the arcades of the sacred wood behind Diotima's garden, where I had seen her for the first time. But what was this? Since then I had so often haunted those trees, had become familiar with them, more at peace under them; now a power laid hold of me, it was as if I stepped within Diana's shadow and must die from the presence of the goddess.

Meanwhile I walked on. With every step the wonder within me grew stronger. I would fain have flown, but it was as if my feet were weighted with lead. My soul had hurried on before and forsaken my earthly limbs. I heard no more, every shape grew dim and tremulous before my eyes. My spirit was already with Diotima; the tree's crown was playing in the light of morning while the lower branches yet felt the chill twilight of dawn.

"Ah! my Hyperion!" a voice now called to me; I flew toward it; "My Diotima! O my Diotima!"—beyond that I had no words and no breath, no consciousness.

Vanish, vanish, mortal life! paltry commerce in which the lone spirit looks ever and again at the pence it has gathered together and counts them over! we are all called to the bliss of the gods!

There is a gap in my existence here. I died, and when I awoke I was lying against the heavenly maiden's heart.

O life of love! in what a ravishing, perfect flowering hadst thou sprung up in her! as if lightly sung to sleep by blessed geniuses, the enchanting head lay on my shoulder, smiling sweet peace, raising eyes the color of the ether to me in happy, innocent amazement, as if they were even now looking at the world for the first time.

Long did we stand thus, ourselves forgotten in lovely contemplation, neither of us knowing what was befalling us, until at last joy increased in me too greatly and my lost speech broke forth in tears and cries of delight and roused my rapt, silent Diotima back to life.

At last we looked around us again.

"O my old, kindly trees!" cried Diotima, as if she had not seen them for a long time, and the memory of her earlier solitary days played over her joys, as charmingly as shadows upon virgin snow when it blushes and burns in the joyous light of sunset.

"Angel from heaven," I cried, "who can conceive you? who can say that he has wholly understood you?"

"Are you surprised," she answered, "that I am so fond

of you? O my proudly humble beloved! Am I, then, one of those who cannot believe in you? have I not fathomed you, not recognized the genius among his clouds? Hide yourself as much as you will, refuse to see yourself; I will conjure you forth, I will—

"But he is already here, he has come forth like a star; he has broken through the husk and stands there like spring; like a crystal rill from a dark cavern, so has he come forth; this is not the somber Hyperion, this is no longer his wild sorrow—O my glorious boy, O mine!"

All this was like a dream to me. Could I believe in such a miracle of love? could I? the joy of it would have killed me.

"Divine creature!" I cried, "is it to me that you speak? can you thus deny yourself, deny your blissful self-sufficiency? can you thus rejoice in me? Oh, now I see, now I know, what I have dimly surmised so often: man is a garment that a god often dons, a cup into which heaven pours its nectar, that its children may taste of the best."

"Yes, yes," she interrupted me, smiling raptly, "your namesake, the glorious Hyperion of the heavens, is in you."

"Let me," I cried, "let me be yours, let me forget myself, let all the life of body and spirit in me fly but to you; but to you, in blissful, endless contemplation! O Diotima! so did I once stand, too, before the shadowy divine image that my love created for itself, before the idol of my lonely dreams; I nourished it faithfully; I animated it with my life, with my heart's hopes I refreshed it, warmed it, but it gave me nothing save what I had given, and when I had become impoverished, it left me poor; and now! now I have you in my arms and I feel the breath of your breast, and feel your eyes in mine, your beautiful presence flows into all my senses, and I can bear it, now I possess all that is most glorious, and tremble no longer, yes! truly I am not he who I was, Diotima! I have become like you, and divinity plays with divinity like children playing together."

"But try to be a little calmer," she said.

"You are right, my lovable one!" I cried joyously; "if

I am not, the Graces do not appear to me; if I am not, I do not see the sweet, subtle movements of Beauty's sea. Oh, I will yet learn to overlook nothing of you. Only give me time!"

"Flatterer!" she cried, "but this must be the end for today, dear flatterer! the golden cloud of evening has given me warning. O be not sad! Preserve this pure joy for you and for me! Let it echo in you until tomorrow, and kill it not with discontent! the heart's flowers need gentle care. Their root is everywhere, but they themselves flourish only in fair weather. Farewell, Hyperion!"

She freed herself. My whole being flamed up in me, as she vanished from me in her glowing beauty.

"O you!" I cried, and flew after her and gave my soul into her hand in endless kisses.

"God!" she cried, "what will come of this?"

That struck home. "Forgive me, divine creature!" I said, "I go. Good night, Diotima! Only think of me a little!"

"I will," she cried, "good night!"

And now not another word, my Bellarmin. It would be too much for my longsuffering heart. I feel I am shaken. But I will go out among the plants and trees and lie down among them and pray that Nature may bring me to a quiet like theirs.

Hyperion to Bellarmin

Our souls now lived ever more freely and beautifully together, and everything in us and about us fused into golden peace. It seemed as if the old world had died and a new were beginning with us, so pure and strong and loving and light had everything become, and we and all that has being floated together in blissful union, like a chorus of a thousand inseparable tones, through the endless ether.

Our conversations glided on like a sky-blue stream from which the golden sand gleams now and again, and our silence was like the silence of the mountain peak, where, in glorious, lofty solitude, high above the realm of storms, only the air of heaven still murmurs through the bold traveler's locks.

And the wondrous, sacred grief, when the hour of parting tolled through our exaltation, and I often cried: "Now we are mortal again, Diotima!" and she said: "Mortality is illusion, is like the colors that quiver before our eyes when they have long looked at the sun"!

Ah! and all the gracious pastimes of love! the cajoling words, the misgivings, the sensitivities, the sternness and indulgence.

And the all-embracing knowledge with which we saw each other through and through, and the infinite trust with which we glorified each other!

Yes, man is a sun, all-seeing and all-illuminating, when he loves; loving not, he is a dark house in which a smoking lamp burns.

I should be silent, should forget and be silent.

But the bewitching flame tempts me until I plunge into it headlong and, like the fly, perish.

Amid all this blessed, unrestrained giving and taking, I one day felt that Diotima was becoming more and more quiet.

I questioned, I implored; but that seemed only to make her yet more distant; finally she implored me to question her no more, to go, and, when I returned, to talk of something else. That cast me, too, into a painful silence, which I found hard to bear.

It was as if an unbelievably sudden fate had vowed the death of our love, and all life was gone, from me and from all else.

I was ashamed of this feeling; I knew very well that chance did not govern Diotima's heart. But what she was remained a mystery to me, and my pampered, disconsolate spirit ever demanded manifest and present love; for it, hidden treasures were lost treasures. Ah! in my happiness I had come to forget hope, at that time I was still like those impatient children who cry for the apple on the tree as if it were not there at all unless it is kissing their lips. I knew no rest, again I implored, violently and meekly, in tenderness and anger, love armed me with all its invincible, humble eloquence, and now—O my Diotima! now I had it, the enchanting confession, I have it now and shall keep it, until the tide of love brings me, too, with all that I am, back to our ancient home, to the bosom of Nature.

What innocence was hers! not yet did she know the power and richness of her heart, and sweetly terrified by the wealth within her, she buried it in the depths of her breast—and when now, with oh! what sacred ingenuousness, she confessed, confessed with tears, that she loved too much, and took leave of all that she had until then cradled against her heart, and cried: "I have become unfaithful to May and summer and autumn, and heed not day and night as once I did, belong no more to Heaven and Earth, belong but to one, to one; but the bloom of May and the flame of summer and the ripeness of autumn, the brightness of day and the solemnity of night, and Earth and Heaven are united for me in that one! so do I love!" and when now, in utter content of heart she looked at me, when, in brave, holy joy, she took me into her beautiful arms and kissed my forehead and my mouth, ha! when that divine head, dying in bliss, sank down against my bared throat, and the sweet lips rested on my beating breast and her lovely breath touched my soul— O Bellarmin! my senses fail me, my spirit flees.

I see, I see how it must end. The rudder has dropped into the tide and the ship, like a child caught by the feet, is seized and flung against the cliffs.

Hyperion to Bellarmin

Life has great hours. We gaze up at them as at the colossal figures of the Future and of Antiquity, we fight a glorious fight with them, and if we hold our own against them, they become like sisters and never forsake us.

Once we were sitting together on our mountain, on a stone of the city that anciently stood on this island, we

were talking together of how the lion Demosthenes found
his end here, how by a sacred, self-sought death, he here
made his way out of Macedonian chains and daggers to
freedom.—"That glorious spirit departed from the world
with a jest," cried one. "Why not?" I said; "there was
nothing left for him here; Athens had become Alexander's
whore, and the world was being chivied to death like a
hart by the great huntsman."

"O Athens!" cried Diotima; "I have more than once
mourned when I looked out thither and the phantom of
the Olympieion rose before me from the blue twilight!"

"How long a crossing is it?" I asked.

"A day's journey, more or less," answered Diotima.

"A day's journey!" I cried, "and I have not yet been
there? We must go across together at once."

"Indeed yes!" cried Diotima; "we shall have a calm
sea tomorrow, and everything is still in its time of green-
ness and ripeness.

"The eternal sun and the life of the immortal earth are
essential for such a pilgrimage."

"Tomorrow, then!" I cried, and our friends assented.

We started early, the cocks were still crowing as we
passed out of the roadstead. The world shone fresh and
bright, and so did we. In our hearts was the golden peace
of youth. The life in us was like the life of a newborn
ocean island, with its first spring just beginning.

Under Diotima's influence, my soul had long since attained more equipoise; today I felt this with threefold
clarity, and my dispersed and roving powers were all concentrated in one golden mean.

We talked of the excellence of the ancient Athenians,
of whence it arose and in what it consisted.

One said that the climate had produced it; another, art
and philosophy; a third, religion and form of government.

"Athenian art and religion, and philosophy and form
of government," said I, "are flowers and fruits of the tree,
not soil and root. You take the effects for the cause.

"But let him who tells me that the climate produced
all this consider that we still live in it ourselves.

"Left more undisturbed in every way, freer from ruthless interference than any other people on earth, so did

the Athenian people grow to manhood. No conqueror weakens them, no success in war intoxicates them, no foreign religion stupefies them, no rash wisdom urges them to premature ripeness. Left to itself, like the forming diamond—such is their childhood. Almost nothing is heard of them until the times of Pisistratus and Hipparchus. They took but a small part in the Trojan War, which, as in a forcing house, too early heated and stimulated most of the Greek peoples.—An extraordinary destiny never begets *men*. The sons of such a mother are great, are giants, but they never become beings of beauty or, what is the same thing, men—or else not until late, when the opposing forces in them battle too savagely not to make peace at last.

"In exuberant vigor Lacedaemon rushes ahead of the Athenians, and for that very reason would have dissipated and dissolved itself, had not Lycurgus come and, for all its overweening nature, held it together by his discipline. From then on everything in the Spartan was an achievement, every excellence was laboriously conquered, bought at the price of conscious effort, and if in a certain sense we can speak of Spartan simplicity, still the true simplicity of the child was completely lacking in them. The Lacedaemonians too early transgressed the order of instinct, they degenerated too soon, hence discipline, too, had likewise to begin for them too early; for every discipline and art begins too early when man's nature has not yet become mature. Nature must have developed to perfection in the human child before he goes to school, so that the image of childhood may show him the way back from school to the perfection of Nature.

"The Spartans forever remained a fragment; for he who was not once a perfect child is hard put to it to become a perfect man.—

"It is true, too, that Heaven and Earth did their part for the Athenians, as for all the Greeks, gave them neither poverty nor superfluity. The rays of Heaven did not fall on them like a rain of fire. Earth did not pamper them, intoxicate them, with caresses and excessive gifts, as the foolish Mother sometimes does elsewhere.

"To add to this, came Theseus' prodigious act, his voluntary limitation of his own royal power.

"Oh! such a seed sown in the hearts of the people cannot but bring forth an ocean of golden ears; and even at this late hour it still visibly operates and flourishes among the Athenians.

"I say it again! That the Athenians grew up so free from every kind of ruthless interference, on so moderate a diet—it was this that made them so outstandingly excellent, and only this could do it!

"Leave the human being undisturbed from the cradle on! do not force him out of the close-wrapped bud of his being, the small house of his childhood! Do not too little, lest he make shift without you, and hence distinguishes you from himself; do not too much, lest he feel your power or his own, and hence distinguishes you from himself; in short, let him not learn until late that there are men, that there is something else outside of himself, for only thus will he become man. But man is a god as soon as he is man. And once he is a god, he is beautiful."

"How strange!" cried one of our friends.

"You have never yet spoken so deeply from my soul," cried Diotima.

"It comes to me from you," I answered.

"It is so that the Athenian was a man," I continued; "and so he could not but become a man. Beautiful he came from Nature's hands, beautiful in body and soul, as the saying goes.

"The first child of human, of divine Beauty is art. In art the divine man rejuvenates and repeats himself. He wants to feel himself, therefore he sets his Beauty over against himself. Thus did man give himself his gods. For in the beginning man and his gods were one, when, unknown to itself, eternal Beauty *was*. I speak mysteries, but they exist.—

"The first child of divine Beauty is art. Thus it was among the Athenians.

"Beauty's second daughter is religion. Religion is love of Beauty. The wise man loves Beauty herself, eternal, all-embracing Beauty; the people love her children, the gods, who appear to them in multifarious forms. So it was, too, among the Athenians. And without such a love of Beauty, without such a religion, every state is a dry skeleton without life and spirit, all thought and action is a tree without a top, a column whose crown has been cut off.

"That this was indeed the case among the Greeks, and especially the Athenians, that their art and their religion were the true children of eternal Beauty—perfect human nature—and could only spring from perfect human nature, is clearly apparent if we will but look with unprejudiced eyes at the productions of their sacred art and at the religion with which they loved and honored them.

"Shortcomings and false steps are to be found everywhere, and hence here too. But it is certain that, even so, in most of the productions of their art we find man in his maturity. Here there is neither the pettiness nor the colossality of the Egyptians and the Goths, here there is human intelligence and human proportions. They run less than other peoples to the extremes of the metaphysical and the physical. Their gods remain more nearly in the golden mean of humanity than others.

"And even as the productions of their art were, so was their love. Not too servile, and not too familiar!—

"This beauty of mind and spirit in the Athenians inevitably produced the indispensable sense of freedom.

"The Egyptian impassively bears the despotism of arbitrary power, the son of the North unprotestingly bears the despotism of law, injustice in the form of codes of justice; for the Egyptian is born from the womb with an urge to do homage, to idolatrize; in the North, men believe too little in the pure, free life of Nature not to cling superstitiously to legality.

"The Athenian cannot tolerate arbitrary power, because his divine nature refuses to be intruded upon, he cannot tolerate legality everywhere because he does not need it everywhere. Draco is not for him! He insists on being treated gently, and he is right to do so."

"Well and good!" someone interrupted me; "I understand this, but I do not see how this poetic and religious people also comes to be a philosophical people."

"The fact is," I answered, "that without poetry they would never have been a philosophical people!"

"What has philosophy," he answered, "what has the cold sublimity of philosophical knowledge, to do with poetry?"

"Poetry," I answered, confident of my argument, "is the beginning and the end of philosophical knowledge. Like Minerva from the head of Jupiter, philosophy springs from the poetry of an eternal, divine state of being. And so in philosophy, too, the irreconcilable finally converges again in the mysterious spring of poetry."

"What a man of paradoxes!" cried Diotima; "yet I divine him. But you two digress. We are talking of Athens."

"The man," I resumed, "who has not at least once in his life felt full, pure beauty in himself, when the powers of his being merged like the colors in the rainbow, who has never felt the profound harmony that arises among all things only in hours of exaltation—that man will not even be a philosophical sceptic, his mind is not even capable of tearing down, let alone of building up. For, believe me, the sceptic finds contradiction and imperfection in all that is thought, because he knows the harmony of perfect beauty, which is never thought. The dry bread that human reason well-meaningly offers him, he disdains only because he is secretly feasting at the table of the gods."

"Visionary!" cried Diotima. "So that is why you, too, were a sceptic. But the Athenians!"

"I am close upon them," I said. "The great saying, the εν διαφερον εαυτω (the one differentiated in itself) of Heraclitus, could be found only by a Greek, for it is the very being of Beauty, and before that was found there was no philosophy.

"Now classification became possible, for the whole was there. The flower had ripened; now it could be dissected.

"The moment of beauty was now well known to men, it was there in life and thought, the infinitely one existed.

"It could be analyzed, taken apart in men's minds, it could be reconstituted from its components, and so the being of the highest and the best could be increasingly known, and the knowledge of it be set up as the law in all the multifarious realms of the spirit.

"Do you see now why the Athenians in particular could not but be a philosophical people too?

"Not so the Egyptian. He who does not live loving Heaven and Earth and loved by them in equal measure, he who does not live at one in this sense with the element in which he has his being, is by his very nature not so at one with himself as a Greek, at least he does not experience eternal Beauty as easily as a Greek does.

"Like a grandiose despot, the East in its power and splendor casts its inhabitants to the ground and, before man has learned to walk, he is forced to kneel, before he has learned to speak, he is forced to pray; before his heart has attained an equipoise it is forced to bow, before his spirit is strong enough to bear flowers and fruit, Fate and Nature drains all his strength through torrid heat. The Egyptian is devoted before he is a whole, hence he knows nothing of the whole, nothing of Beauty, and what he calls the highest is a veiled power, an awesome enigma; the dumb, dark Isis is his first and last, an empty infinity, and out of that nothing reasonable has ever come. Even the most sublime nothingness gives birth to nothingness.

"The North, on the contrary, too early turns its nurslings in upon themselves; and if the spirit of the fiery Egyptian hurries forth too eagerly to journey through the world, in the North the spirit begins to return into itself even before it is ready to travel.

"In the North one must be judicious before one's capacity for feeling has fully developed, one thinks oneself guilty of everything even before ingenuousness has achieved its beautiful end; one must be reasonable, must become a conscious intelligence before one is a man, be a shrewd man before one is a child; the oneness of the whole man, Beauty, is not allowed to thrive and ripen in him before he cultivates and develops himself. Pure intellect, pure reason are always the kings of the North.

"But pure intellect has never produced anything intelligent, nor pure reason anything reasonable.

"Without beauty of spirit, intellect is like a willing journeyman who carpenters the fence out of rough timber as it has been sketched out for him and nails the sawn and planed palings together for the garden that his master intends to plant. The entire business of intellect is make-shift. By its ability to sort out, it saves us from folly, from injustice; but to be safe from folly and injustice is, after all, not the highest level of human excellence.

"Reason without beauty of spirit and heart is like an overseer whom the master of the house has set over the servants; he knows as little as they do what will come of all their endless toil, he only shouts: 'Bestir yourselves,' and is almost sorry to find the work being accomplished, for in the end he would have nothing more to oversee, and his part would be played.

"Mere intellect produces no philosophy, for philosophy is more than the limited perception of what is.

"Mere reason produces no philosophy, for philosophy is more than the blind demand for ever greater progress in the combination and differentiation of some particular material.

"But once the light of the divine εν διαφερον εαυτῳ, which is struggling reason's ideal of Beauty, shines out, it does not demand blindly, it knows why and to what end it demands.

"If the sun of the Beautiful shines for intellect at its work, as a May day shines into the artist's workshop, it does not go running out and leave its work of makeshift unfinished, though it thinks fondly of the holiday when it will rove abroad in the rejuvenating light of spring."

Thus far had I discoursed, when we landed on the shore of Attica.

Ancient Athens was now too much in our minds for us to engage in anything like an orderly conversation; and I now felt surprised myself at the sort of things I had been saying. "How did I ever come," I cried, "to be on the arid mountain peak on which you saw me just now?"

"It is ever thus," Diotima answered, "when we feel at our best. Exuberant strength seeks something to do. Young lambs butt their heads together when they are sated with their mother's milk."

We made our way to the summit of Lycabettus, and, though pressed for time, we stopped now and again wrapped in thought, preparing ourselves for wonders to come.

It is beautiful that man finds it so hard to convince

himself of the death of what he loves; probably no one has ever visited a friend's grave without some faint hope of really finding his friend there. The beautiful phantom of ancient Athens took possession of me like the figure of a mother returning from the realm of the dead.

"O Parthenon!" I cried, "pride of the world! Neptune's kingdom lies at thy feet like a subjugated lion, and around thee the other temples cluster like children, and the eloquent Agora and the Grove of Academe—"

"Can you thus transport yourself to ancient times?" asked Diotima.

"Remind me not of time!" I answered; "it was a divine life and in it man was the center of Nature. Spring, when it blossomed about Athens, was like a modest flower on a maiden's bosom; the sun rose red with shame before the glories of earth.

"The marble cliffs of Hymettus and Pentelicus leaped from their slumbering cradle like children from their mother's lap, and attained form and life under the loving hands of Athenians.

"Nature bestowed honey and the most beautiful violets and myrtles and olives.

"Nature was a priestess and man her god, and all life in her and her every form and sound were but a single rapt echo of that glorious one to whom she belonged.

"Him did she celebrate, to him only did she sacrifice.

"And he was worthy of it, whether he sat fondly in the sacred workshop clasping the knees of the divine image that he had fashioned, or lay at ease among his listening students on Sunium's green promontory, whiling away the time with high thoughts, or ran in the Stadium, or, from the orator's tribune, sent rain and sunshine and thunder and golden clouds, like the Storm God—"

"Oh, look!" Diotima suddenly cried to me.

I looked, and could have fainted, so mighty was the spectacle.

Like an immense shipwreck, when the gales have been hushed and the sailors have fled and the corpse of the shattered fleet lies on the sandbank unrecognizable, so before us lay Athens, and the forsaken pillars stood before us like the bare treetrunks of a wood that at evening was still green and, the same night, went up in flames.

"Here," said Diotima, "one learns to accept one's own fate in silence, be it good or bad."

"Here," I continued, "one learns to accept all things in silence. Had the reapers who mowed this grainfield enriched their barns with its stalks, nothing would have been lost, and I should be content to stand here as a gleaner —but who was the gainer?"

"The whole of Europe," answered one of our friends.

"Oh, yes!" I cried, "they have dragged away the columns and statues and sold them to one another, they have put no small price on those noble forms—for their rarity, as one prizes parrots and monkeys."

"Say not so," the same man answered; "if it is indeed true that the spirit of all that beauty is not among them, it is because it could not be carried away, could not be bought."

"Yes," I cried, "yes! That spirit had perished even before the destroyers descended on Attica. Not until houses and temples have been deserted do the wild beasts dare to venture into gateways and streets."

"For him who possesses that spirit," said Diotima consolingly, "Athens still stands like a blossoming fruit tree. The artist can easily restore the torso for himself."

The next morning we set out early, saw the ruins of the Parthenon, the site of the ancient Theater of Dionysus, the Temple of Theseus, the sixteen still-standing pillars of the divine Olympieion; but what struck me most was the ancient gate that in times past afforded passage from the old city to the new, where once a thousand beautiful men and women must have greeted each other in a single day. Now the gate gives passage to neither the old nor the new city, it stands there silent and empty, like a dried up fountain from whose conduits clear, cool water once jetted with a welcoming plash.

"Ah!" said I as we walked about, "Fate makes brave sport here, throwing down temples and giving their shattered stones to children to play with, turning disfigured gods into benches before peasants' huts, and tombs into resting places for pasturing cattle; such prodigality is more royal than Cleopatra's whim of drinking the dissolved pearl—but alas for all that beauty and greatness!"

"Dear Hyperion!" cried Diotima, "it is time for you to go from here; you are pale, your eyes are tired, and you seek in vain to sustain yourself with new thoughts. Come out where it is green! out among the colors of life! That will do you good."

We went out into the nearby gardens.

The others, having fallen into talk with two English scholars who were reaping a harvest from the antiquities of Athens, were not to be budged. I was glad to leave them.

My whole being revived when I found myself alone with Diotima again; she had fought a magnificent fight against the sacred chaos of Athens. As the lyre of Urania above the discordant elements, so Diotima's quiet thoughts ruled above the ruins. As the moon out of a tenuous cloud-bank, so her spirit rose out of her beautiful sorrow; the divine maiden stood there in her grief like the flower that breathes forth its loveliest perfume in the dark of night.

We walked on and on, and at last had not walked in vain.

O ye groves of Angele, where the olive tree and the cypress, whispering together, cool each other with pleasant shade, where the golden fruit of the lemon tree glimmers from among dark leaves, where the swelling grape grows luxuriantly on the stake, and the ripe bitter-orange lies by the wayside like a smiling foundling! ye sweet-scented, hidden paths, ye peaceful seats, where the reflection of the myrtle smiles out of the spring! never shall I forget you.

Diotima and I walked about for a while under the glorious trees, until we came upon a bright open expanse.

Here we sat down. There was a blissful silence between us. My spirit fluttered about the maiden's divine form like a butterfly about a flower, and my whole being was eased and brought to harmony in the joy of inspiring contemplation.

"Are you so soon comforted, scatterbrain?" said Diotima.

"Yes, yes, I am!" I answered. "What I thought was

lost, I have; what I pined for as if it had vanished from the world, is here before me. No, Diotima! the spring of eternal Beauty has not yet dried up.

"I have said it to you before: I need gods and men no longer. I know that Heaven is desolate, depopulated, and that Earth, which once overflowed with beautiful human life, is become almost like an anthill. But there is still a place where the old Heaven and the old Earth smile for me. For the gods of Heaven and the godlike men of the Earth—I forget them all in you.

"What care I for the shipwreck of the world, I know nothing but my blessed island."

"There is a time for love," said Diotima with gentle seriousness, "as there is a time to live in the happy cradle. But life itself drives us forth.

"Hyperion!"—here she ardently grasped my hand, and her voice rose grandly—"Hyperion! I think you are born for higher things. Do not misjudge yourself! it was lack of material that held you back. Things went too slowly. That cast you down. Like young fencers, you attacked too soon, before your aim was certain and your hand skilled; and because, as was bound to happen, you took more thrusts than you gave, you became timid and doubted yourself and everything else; for you are as sensitive as you are impetuous. But that has lost you nothing. If your heart and your capacity for action had matured so early, your spirit would not be what it is; you would not be the thinking man, would not be the suffering, turbulent man. Believe me, you would never have known the equipoise of beautiful humanity so purely if you had not lost it so completely. Your heart has at last found peace. I believe it. I understand it. But do you truly think that you have reached the end? Do you mean to shut yourself up in the heaven of your love, and let the world, which needs you, wither and grow cold before you? You must shoot down like the beam of light, you must descend like the all-refreshing rain, into the land of mortal men, you must illuminate like Apollo, shake and animate like Jupiter, or you are not worthy of your heaven. I beg you: go back into Athens again, and look not only at the ruins but also at the men who walk among them, the wild Albanians and the other good-hearted, childlike Greeks, who console themselves with a merry dance and a pious tale for the infamous oppression that weighs upon them—can you say, 'I am ashamed to work with this material?' I think it can still be fashioned. Can you turn your heart from those who are in need? They are not evil, they have done you no harm!"

"What can I do for them?" I cried.

"Give them what you have within you," answered Diotima, "give—"

"Not another word, noble soul!" I cried, "else you will bend me, else it will be as if you had brought me to it by force—

"They will not be happier, but nobler—no! they will be happier too. They must arise, they must come forth, like young mountains out of the ocean when their underground fire drives them.

"It is true that I stand alone, and appear among them without a name. But cannot one alone, if he is a man, do more than hundreds who are but fragments of men?

"Sacred Nature, thou art the same within me and without. It cannot be so hard to unite what is outside of me and the divine within me. If the bee can make her little kingdom flourish, why should not I be able to plant and cultivate what is needful?

"What! the Arabian merchant sowed his Koran abroad, and a people of scholars grew up for him like an endless forest; and shall the field not thrive to which ancient truth returns in new, living youth?

"All shall be changed! From the root of humanity the new world shall spring! A new divinity shall rule over them, a new future brighten before them.

"In the workshop, in houses, in gatherings, in temples —there will be a change everywhere!

"But I must still go away and learn. I am an artist, and I am unskilled. I fashion in thought, but I do not yet know how to direct my hand—"

"You shall go to Italy," said Diotima, "to Germany, France—how many years do you need? three? four?—I think three are enough; you are no slowcoach, and you seek only what is noblest and most beautiful—"

"And then?"

"You will be the teacher of our people, you will be a great man, I hope. And when then, as now, I embrace you, I shall dream, as if I were a part of a glorious man, I shall rejoice, as if you had given me half of your immortality, even as Castor did to Pollux, oh! I shall be a proud girl, Hyperion!"

I remained silent for a while. I was filled with inexpressible joy.

"Is it possible that there is content between the decision and the act, is there rest before the victory?"

"It is the rest of the hero," said Diotima, "there are decisions that, like the words of gods, are at once command and fulfillment, and such is yours."

We returned, as after our first embrace. Everything had become strange and new for us.

Now I stood above the ruins of Athens like the farmer on the fallow field. "Only lie still," I thought, as we returned to our ship, "only lie still, sleeping land! Soon will the young life sprout green from thee and grow toward the blessings of Heaven! Soon will the clouds never rain in vain, soon will the Sun find his old nurslings once more.

"Thou askest for men, Nature? Thou complainest, like a lyre on which only that brother of chance, the wind, plays because the artist who imposed order on it has died? They will come, thy men, O Nature! A rejuvenated people will rejuvenate thee, too, and thou wilt be as its bride, and the old union of spirits will renew itself in thee.

"There will be but one Beauty; and man and Nature will be united in one all-embracing divinity."

PART TWO

μη φυναι, τον απαντα νικα λογον. το δ'επει
φανη βηναι κειθεν, οθεν περ ηκει, πολυ δευτερον
ως ταχιστα.

SOPHOCLES

[NOT TO BE BORN IS, PAST ALL PRIZING, BEST;
BUT, WHEN A MAN HAS SEEN THE LIGHT, THIS
IS NEXT BEST BY FAR, THAT WITH ALL SPEED
HE SHOULD GO THITHER, WHENCE HE HATH
COME.]

BOOK ONE

Hyperion to Bellarmin

We were experiencing the last beautiful moments of the year, after our return from Attica.

Autumn was a brother of spring for us, full of mild fire, a festival time for memories of sorrows and past joys of love. The fading leaves bore the rosy hue of sunset, only the spruce and the laurel stood in eternal green. Migrating birds lingered in the clear air, others swarmed in vineyard and garden, joyously reaping what men had left. And the heavenly light ran pure from the cloudless sky, the sacred sun smiled through every twig—the kindly one, never named by me but with joy and gratitude, the sun that with a look has often healed me in deep sorrow, and cleansed my soul of discontent and cares.

We visited all our best loved paths once more, Diotima and I; vanished blissful hours met us everywhere.

We remembered the past May; never, we said, had we seen the Earth as it was then; it had been transformed, a silver cloud of flowers, a joyous flame of life, purified of all grosser matter.

"Oh! all was so full of pleasure and hope," cried Diotima, "so full of unceasing growth and yet so effortless, so blessedly quiet, like a child playing on and on without another thought."

"In that," I cried, "I recognize the soul of Nature—in that still fire, in that lingering in its mighty haste."

"And how dear it is to the happy, that lingering," cried

Diotima; "do you remember? once at twilight we stood together on the bridge, after a hard storm, and the red mountain stream shot away under us like an arrow, but there beside it the forest stood in green peace and the bright leaves scarcely stirred. We felt so glad then that the living green did not flee from us too, like the brook, and that the beautiful spring stayed for us like a tame bird; yet now spring, too, is over the hills and away."

We smiled at that, although sorrow was closer to us.

So was our own bliss to depart, and we foresaw it.

O Bellarmin! who shall dare to say that he stands fast, when even the beautiful thus ripens to its doom, when even the divine must humble itself and share mortality with all that is mortal!

Hyperion to Bellarmin

I had lingered before her house with the lovely maid, until the lamp of night shone into the peaceful twilight; then I returned to Notara's dwelling, full of thoughts, full of seething, heroic life, as always when I left her embraces. A letter had come from Alabanda.

"Things are stirring, Hyperion," he wrote to me, "Russia has declared war on the Porte; they are bringing a fleet into the Archipelago;* the Greeks are to be free if they rise and help drive the Sultan to the Euphrates. The Greeks will do their share, the Greeks will be free, and I am heartily glad that at last there is something to do again. I took no pleasure in the light of day, so long as this remained undone.

"If you are still what you were, come! You will find me in the village before Coron as you come by the road from Mistra. I live beside the hill, in the white house at the edge of the woods.

"I have broken with the men whom you met through me in Smyrna. You were right, with your finer sensitivity, not to enter their sphere.

* In the year 1770 [Hölderlin's note].

beautiful Soul

"I long for us to see each other again in the new life. Until now, you have seen the world as too evil for you to let it know you. Because you refused to perform servile tasks, you did nothing, and doing nothing made you morose and dreamy.

"You refused to swim in the swamp. Come now, come, and let us bathe in the open sea!

"It will do us good, O you whom alone I love!"

So he wrote. For a moment I was aghast. My face burned with shame, my heart seethed like hot springs, and I could not stand still, such anguish did I feel at being outdistanced by Alabanda, outdone forever. But then I all the more eagerly embraced the work before us.

"I have grown too idle," I cried, "too fond of my ease, too remote, too inactive!—Alabanda looks into the world like a noble pilot, Alabanda is diligent and searches the waves for booty; and do your hands sleep on your lap? would you make do with words, and exorcise the world with magic spells? But your words are like snowflakes, useless, they only make the air darker, and your magic formulas are for believers, but the unbelievers do not hear you.—Yes! to be mild at the right time is a fine thing, but to be mild at the wrong time is ugly, for it is cowardly!—But, Harmodius! I will match thy myrtle, thy myrtle, in which the sword lay hidden. I will not have been idle for nothing, and my sleep shall be like oil when flame touches it. I will not look on when the time is at hand, will not go about asking for news while Alabanda earns the laurel."

Hyperion to Bellarmin

Diotima's increasing pallor as she read Alabanda's letter pierced my soul. She then began, calmly and earnestly, to advise me against the step, and we said many things for and against it. "O men of violence!" she cried at last, "who so quickly go to extremes, think of Nemesis!"

"He who suffers extremes," I said, "is right to go to extremes."

"Even if it is right," she said, "you were not born for it."

"So it seems," I said; "but I have dallied long enough. Oh, would that I could load an Atlas upon me, to make good the sins of my youth. Is there consciousness in me? is there endurance? Oh, let me, Diotima! Here, in just such work, must I gain it."

"This is vain pride!" cried Diotima; "not long ago you were more modest, not long ago when you said, 'I must still go away and learn.'"

"Dear sophist!" I cried; "then we were talking of something entirely different. To lead my people to the Olympus of divine Beauty, where Truth and all Goodness gushes from springs forever young—I am not yet fit to do that. But I have learned to use a sword, and for the moment that is all that is needed. The new union of spirits cannot live in the air, the sacred theocracy of the Beautiful must dwell in a free state, and that state must have a place on earth, and that place we shall surely conquer."

"You will conquer," cried Diotima, "and forget what for; you will, at the most, force the establishment of a free state, and then ask yourself, 'What have I been building for?' Ah! it will be consumed, all the beautiful life that was to have being there, it will be exhausted even in you! The savage fight will tear you to pieces, beautiful soul, you will grow old, blissful spirit! and, weary unto death, you will ask in the end: 'Where are ye now, ye ideals of youth?'"

"It is cruel, Diotima," I cried, "thus to reach into my very heart, thus to hold me fast by my own fear of death, by my highest joy in life; but no! no! no! Servitude kills, but just war brings every soul to life. It is casting the gold into the fire that gives it the color of the sun! It is breaking fetters that first gives a man all his youth! It is arising and trampling on the adder, on the crawling century that poisons all Beauty and Nature in the bud— that alone saves a man!—I shall grow old, shall I, Diotima, setting Greece free? grow old and miserable, become a common man? Oh, then was he, too, shallow and empty and forsaken of the gods, that Athenian youth, when, bearing news of victory from Marathon, he came over the peak of Pentelicus and looked down into the valleys of Attica!"

"My love! my love!" cried Diotima, "oh, be still! I will not say another word. You shall go, shall go, proud man! Ah! when you are thus, I have no power over you, no right to you."

She wept bitterly, and I stood before her like a criminal. "Forgive me, divine maid!" I cried, kneeling at her feet, "oh, forgive me, when I am compelled! I do not choose, I do not reflect. There is a power in me, and I know not if it is myself that drives me to this step." "Your whole soul commands you to it," she answered. "Not to obey one's soul ofttimes leads to destruction, yet obeying it does too. It is best that you go, for it is nobler. Act; I will bear it."

Hyperion to Bellarmin

From then on Diotima was strangely changed.

I had seen with joy how, from the time we loved, her silent life had opened into looks and fond words and her inborn quietude had often met me with shining enthusiasm.

But oh! how strange the beautiful soul becomes to us, when, after its first blossoming, after the morning of its course, it must rise to its high noon! The blessed child had grown almost unrecognizable, so sublime and so sorrowful had she become.

Oh, how often did I lie before that divine, mourning figure, and thought that I should weep my soul away in grief for her, and then myself rose up in admiration and filled with unconquerable powers! A flame had ascended into her eyes from her full heart. Her bosom, teeming with longings and sorrows, had become too confining for her; that is why her thoughts were so glorious and bold. A new greatness, a visible power over everything that could feel, ruled in her. She was a higher being. She belonged to the race of mortals no longer.

O my Diotima, if I had thought then to what this must come!

Hyperion to Bellarmin

The prudent Notara, too, was enchanted by the new projects, promised me a strong following, hoped soon to occupy the Isthmus of Corinth and there take Greece as it were by the handle. But Fate decreed otherwise, and made his work useless before it achieved its end.

He advised me not to go to Tina, but to travel directly down the Peloponnesus, escaping notice as far as possible. I was to write to my father on the way, since the cautious old man would more easily condone a step that had been taken than give permission for one that had not. This was not quite to my taste, but we are prone to sacrifice our private feelings when a great goal is before our eyes.

"I doubt," Notara continued, "if you will be able to count on your father's help in a matter of this sort. So I shall give you what you will need in order to live and work for a time, come what may. If you are ever able to, you can repay me; if not, what was mine was yours as well. Feel no embarrassment about the money," he added with a smile; "even Phoebus' horses do not live on air alone, so the poets tell us."

Hyperion to Bellarmin

And now the day of parting came.

I had spent the whole morning up in Notara's garden, in the fresh winter air, among the ever green cypresses and cedars. The great powers of youth supported me, and my premonition of suffering to come bore me higher, like a cloud.

Diotima's mother had invited Notara and our other friends and myself to pass that last day together at her house. Their kind hearts had all rejoiced over me and Diotima, and the element of the divine in our love had not been lost on them. And now they were to bless my parting too.

I went down, I found the dear girl at the hearth. She took it as a sacred, priestly duty to attend to the house-keeping that day. She had put everything to rights, had beautified everything in the house, and no one was allowed to help her with it. She had gathered all the flowers that still remained in the garden, she had brought roses and fresh bunches of grapes, even at that late time of year.

She recognized my footstep as I approached, she came softly toward me; her pale cheeks were aglow from the fire of the hearth, and her eyes, larger in her new serious-ness, were bright with tears. She saw how overcome I was. "Go inside, my dear," she said; "Mother is there, and I will follow at once."

I went in. There she sat, the noble woman, and held out her beautiful hand to me. "Are you come, are you come, my son?" she cried. "I ought to be angry with you, you have taken my child from me, have talked me out of all common sense, do just what you please and then go away; but forgive him, ye Heavenly Powers, if what he means to do is wrong! and if it is right, then be not slow to help the dear lad!" I was going to speak, but just then Notara and our other friends came in, with Diotima be-hind them.

We were silent for a while. We honored the grieving love that was in us all, we feared to presume upon it with words and arrogant thoughts. Finally, after a few desultory remarks, Diotima asked me to tell them some-thing about Agis and Cleomenes; I had often named those great souls with ardent respect and had said that they were no less demigods than Prometheus, and their battle against Sparta's fate more heroic than any in the most illustrious myths. The genius of those men, I had said, was the sunset of the Greek day, as Theseus and Homer had been its dawn.

I told their story, and at its end we all felt stronger and more exalted.

"Happy is he," cried one of our friends, "whose life alternates between joy of heart and brisk battle!"

"Yes!" cried another, "that is eternal youth, when enough powers are always in exercise and our whole selves are occupied in pleasure and work."

"Oh, that I could go with you!" Diotima cried to me.

"Yet it is fitting that you remain here, Diotima!" said I. "The priestess may not leave the temple. You guard the sacred flame, in silence you guard the Beautiful, that I may find it again in you."

"You are right of course, it is better," she said, and her voice trembled and the ether-blue eyes hid themselves in her handkerchief, that their tears, their despair might not be seen.

O Bellarmin, my heart was near to breaking because I had made her blush so red. "Friends!" I cried, "preserve this angel for me. I know nothing more, if I know her not. O Heavens! I dare not think for what I would be fit if I lost her."

"Rest easy, Hyperion!" Notara interrupted me.

"Easy?" I cried; "O you good people, you can often give thought to how your garden will bloom and how good your harvest will be, you can pray for your grape-vine—and shall I part without concern from what alone my soul serves?"

"No, my good friend!" cried Notara, deeply moved, "no! I do not ask that you part from her without concern, no, by the divine innocence of your love! you have my blessing, be sure of that!"

"You remind me," I cried quickly. "She shall bless us, this dear mother, she shall bear witness for us with you all—come, Diotima, your mother shall bless our union, until the beautiful society for which we hope joins us in marriage."

I went down on one knee; and she, wide-eyed, blushing, smiling, and festive, sank down at my side too

"Long," I cried, "O Nature! has our life been at one with thee, and the world that is ours is divinely young, like thee and all thy gods, through the power of love."

"In thy groves we wandered," Diotima continued, "and were like thee, by thy springs we sat and were like thee, there over the mountains we went, with thy children the stars, like thee."

"When we were far from each other," I cried, "when, like a whispering harp, our coming delight first sounded for us, when we found each other, when there was no more sleep for us, and all the tones in us awoke to the full harmony of life, divine Nature! then were we ever like thee, and so now, too, when we part and joy dies, we are like thee, full of sorrow, yet good; therefore a pure mouth shall bear witness for us that our love is holy and eternal, as thou art."

"I bear witness to it," her mother said.

"We bear witness to it," cried the others.

Now there was no word left for us to speak. I felt my heart beat its highest, I felt ripe for departure. "Now I will go, my loved ones," I said, and life vanished from every face. Diotima stood like a marble statue and I felt her hand die in mine. I had killed everything around me, I was alone, and I reeled before the boundless silence in which my seething life had no holdfast.

"Ah!" I cried, "my heart is fiery hot, and you all stand so coldly, my loved ones! and do only the Gods of the household lend ear?—Diotima! you are silent, you do not see!—oh, well for you that you do not see!"

"Go now," she sighed, "it must be; go now, dear heart!"

"O sweet music from those blissful lips!" I cried, and stood like a suppliant before that lovely statue, "sweet music! drift upon me once more, dawn once more, dear eyes of light!"

"Speak not so, beloved!" she cried, "speak to me more seriously, speak to me with more heart!"

I wanted to restrain myself, but I was as in a dream.

"Alas!" I cried, "it is no parting from which there is a return."

"You will kill her," cried Notara. "See how gentle she is, and you are so beside yourself."

I looked at her, and tears poured from my burning eyes.

"Farewell, then, Diotima!" I cried, "heaven of my love,

farewell!—Let us be strong, dear friends! Dear Mother, I gave you joy and sorrow. Farewell, farewell!"

I staggered away. Diotima alone followed me.

Evening had come, and the stars were rising in the sky. We stopped and stood below the house. There was an eternity within us, above us. Delicate as the ether, Diotima embraced me. "Silly! what is parting?" she whispered mysteriously, with the smile of an immortal.

"I feel differently now, too," I said, "and I do not know which of the two is a dream—my grief or my happiness."

"Both are," she answered, "and both are good."

"Perfect one!" I cried, "I speak as you do. Let us know each other by the starry sky. Let that be the sign between me and you, so long as our lips are dumb."

"So be it!" she said, with a lingering tone that I had never heard before—it was her last. Her image vanished from me in the twilight, and I do not know if it was really she when I turned back for the last time and the fading figure hovered before my eyes a moment longer and then died into the night.

Hyperion to Bellarmin

Why do I recount my grief to you, renew it, and stir up my restless youth in me again? Is it not enough to have traveled once through mortality? why do I not remain still in the peace of my spirit?

It is, my Bellarmin, because every living breath that we draw remains dear to our heart, because all the transformations of pure Nature are part of her beauty too. Our soul, when it puts off mortal experiences and lives only in blessed quietness—is it not like a leafless tree? like a head without locks? Dear Bellarmin! I was quiet for a while; like a child, I lived under the still knolls of Salamis, oblivious to mankind's fate and striving. Since then much has changed in my eyes, and now I have peace enough in me to remain quiet when I look into human existence.

O friend! in the end the Spirit reconciles us with all things. You will not believe it, at least not of me. But I think that even my letters should suffice to show you that my soul is becoming stiller every day. And I will continue to tell you of it hereafter, until I have said enough for you to believe me.

Here are letters of Diotima's and mine, which we wrote to each other after my departure from Calaurea. They are the most precious part of all that I entrust to you. They are the warmest picture from those days of my life. They tell you little of the clamor of war. But hence all the more of my own life, and that is what you want. And, ah! you must see, too, how greatly I was loved. That I could never tell you, that only Diotima can tell.

Hyperion to Diotima

I have awakened from the death of absence, my Diotima! my spirit arises, strengthened, as from sleep.

I write to you from a summit in the mountains of Epidaurus. There, far in the distance, your island looms faintly, Diotima! out there, my stadium, where I must conquer or fall. O Peloponnesus! O ye springs of the Eurotas and Alpheus! There we shall prove ourselves. There, from the forests of Sparta, the ancient genius of the land will plunge down like an eagle with our army, as on roaring pinions.

My soul is filled with longing for high deeds and filled with love, Diotima, and in these Greek valleys my eye looks out as if to command by magic: "Rise once more, ye cities of the gods!"

There must be a god in me, for I scarcely feel our separation. Like the blessed shades by Lethe, my soul now lives with yours in heavenly freedom and Fate has no more power over our love.

Hyperion to Diotima

I am now deep in the Peloponnesus. In the same hut where I spent last night I once spent the night when, scarcely more than a boy, I traveled through these regions with Adamas. How happily I sat here then, on the bench in front of the house, listening to the bells of arriving caravans tinkling in the distance and the plash of the nearby spring, which poured its silver waters into the basin under flowering acacias.

Now I am less happy, I rove through this land as through Dodona's grove, where the oaks resounded with oracles prophesying fame. I see only deeds, past and to come, even though I wander from morning to night under the open sky. Believe me, he who travels through this land and still tolerates a yoke on his neck, still becomes no Pelopidas—he is empty-hearted or without understanding.

Can this sleep have lasted so long? so long has time, dark and dumb as the River of Hell, glided on in drear sloth?

And yet all is ready. The mountain folk hereabout are full of vengeful energy, they lie like a silent storm cloud that waits only for the wind to drive it on. Diotima! let me breathe the breath of God among them, let me speak a word to them from my heart, Diotima. Fear not! They will not be so savage. I know untutored nature. It scorns reason, but it is close kin to enthusiasm. He who but works with his whole soul never goes wrong. He need not ponder, for no power is against him.

Hyperion to Diotima

Tomorrow I shall be with Alabanda. It is a delight to me to ask the way to Coron, and I ask oftener than I need to. I would fain take the wings of the sun and be off to him, yet I find myself inclined to hang back and ask, "What will he be like?"

The kingly youth! why was I born after him? why did I not spring from one cradle with him? I cannot bear the difference between us. Oh, why did I live in Tina like an idle shepherd boy, and did not even dream of such a man as he until he was already testing Nature by living work, already battling sea and air and all the elements? was not a longing for the glory of action astir in me then too?

But I will catch up with him, I will be speedy. By Heaven! I am overripe for work. My soul has only itself to be angry with if I do not soon free myself by some living action.

Noble maiden! how could you not find me wanting? How could you possibly love a being so empty of deeds?

Hyperion to Diotima

I have him, dear Diotima!

My breast is light, and swift my sinews, ha! and the future tempts me, as clear deep water tempts us to leap into it and cool our exuberant blood in that freshening bath. But this is idle chatter. We are dearer to each other than ever, my Alabanda and I. We are freer together, and yet all the fullness and depth of life is there, as it used to be.

Oh, how right the tyrants of old were to forbid such friendships as ours! Then a man is as strong as a demigod and tolerates no insolence within his sphere!—

It was evening when I entered his room. He had just laid aside his work and was sitting by the window in a moonlit corner, communing with his thoughts. I was standing in the dark, he did not recognize me, he looked toward me unconcernedly. Heaven knows who he took me to be. "Well, how goes it?" he cried. "Well enough," I said. But my dissembling availed nothing. My voice was filled with

secret delight. "What is this?" he sprang up; "is it you?"
"Yes, you blindman," I cried, and flew into his arms.
"Oh, now," Alabanda cried at last, "now everything will
be different, Hyperion!"

"So I think too," said I, and happily shook his hand.

"And do you still know me," Alabanda continued after
a time, "have you still your old devout belief in Alabanda?
Magnanimous Hyperion! things have not gone as well for
me since, as they did when I felt the light of your love
on me."

"What!" I cried, "can Alabanda ask this? There was
no pride in those words, Alabanda. But it is a sign of
this age that the old heroic nature goes begging for respect
and the living human heart pines for a drop of love, like
an orphan."

"Dear youth!" he cried; "I have grown old, that is all.
The slackness of life everywhere, and that matter of the
old men to whom I wanted to put you to school in
Smyrna—"

"Oh, it is bitter," I cried; "the deadly Goddess, the
Nameless One whom men call Fate, has not spared even
this man."

Lights were brought, and again we looked at each other,
in cautiously loving scrutiny. My dear friend's figure had
changed very much since those days of hope. His great,
ever animated eye shone upon me from his faded face
like the midday sun from a pallid heaven.

"Dear youth!" cried Alabanda, lovingly vexed to find
me staring at him so, "enough of these dolorous looks,
dear youth! I know very well that I have sunk. O my
Hyperion! I long so much for something great and true
and, with you, I hope to find it. You have outgrown me,
you are freer and stronger than in the past, and, believe
me! it rejoices my heart. I am the parched land, and
you come like a fortunate storm—oh, it is glorious that
you are here!"

"Stop!" I said, "you drive me out of my senses, and we
should not talk of ourselves at all until we are in the
midst of life, among deeds."

"Yes, yes!" Alabanda cried joyously, "not until the
hunting horn sounds do the hunters feel themselves."

"Will it start soon, then?" I said.

"It will," cried Alabanda, "and I tell you, dear heart! it will be quite a fire. Ha! may it reach to the tower's top and melt its vane and rage and swirl about it until it bursts and falls!—and you must not take offense at our allies. I know that the good Russians would like to use us as they do firearms. But let that pass! when our strong Spartans have once learned in the field who they are and of what they are capable, when once we have conquered the Peloponnesus with them, then we will laugh in the North Pole's face and make a life of our own."

"A life of our own," I cried, "a new, an honorable life. Were we born of the swamp, like a will-o'-the-wisp, or are we descended from the victors at Salamis? How is this? how, O free nature of the Greeks, hast thou become a maidservant? how art thou so sunken, ancestral race, of which the divine images of Jupiter and Apollo were once only the copy?—But hear me, sky of Ionia! hear me, my native soil, thou that, half naked, clothest thyself like a beggarwoman in the rags of thine ancient glory, I will bear it no longer!"

"O Sun, who fostered us!" cried Alabanda, "thou shalt witness it when our courage grows under our toil, when our resolution takes shape under the blows of Fate like iron under the hammer."

Each of us fired the other.

"And let no blot remain, none of the abject nonsense with which this century would bedaub us as the rabble do the walls!" "Oh," cried Alabanda, "that is the reason war is so good—"

"Yes, yes, Alabanda," I cried, "even as are all great undertakings, in which men's strength and spirit, not crutches and wings of wax, are the means. There we put off the slaves' clothing branded with the mark which Fate would set upon us—"

"There all that is frivolous, all that is forced has no more currency, we go stripped of ornaments as of chains, naked as in the races at Nemea, straight to the goal."

"To the goal," I cried, "where the young free state dawns and the pantheon of all Beauty arises from the soil of Greece."

Alabanda was silent for a while. A new red rose into his face and his stature waxed upward, like the plant refreshed.

"O Youth, Youth!" he cried, "then will I drink from thy spring, then will I live and love. I am very joyful, Sky of Night," he went on as if intoxicated, walking to the window, "thy vault is over me like the foliage of a vine and thy stars hang down like clusters of grapes."

Hyperion to Diotima

It is my good fortune that my life is completely occupied with work. I should fall into one folly after another, so full is my soul, so am I intoxicated by the proud, the wonderful man who loves nothing but me and heaps all the humility that is in him upon me alone. O Diotima, this Alabanda has wept before me, has begged me like a child to forgive him for what he did to me in Smyrna.

Who am I, you loved ones, that I call you mine, that I dare to say, "They are my own," that, like a conqueror, I stand between you and hold you as my booty?

O Diotima! O Alabanda! noble, calmly great beings! how much there is for me to accomplish, if I am not to flee from my happiness, from you?

Just now, while I was writing, I received your letter, dear one.

Grieve not, lovely being, grieve not! Preserve yourself, unwithered by sorrow, for the future festivals of our country! Diotima, preserve yourself for the shining celebration of Nature and for all the serene days set aside to honor the gods!

Do you not see Greece already?

Oh, do you not see how, rejoicing in their new neighbor, the eternal stars smile over our towns and groves, how the ancient ocean, when it sees our people wandering happily along the shore, remembers the beautiful Athenians and speeds good fortune to us again, as then it did to its favorites, on rejoicing waves?

O soul, O maiden! you are so beautiful already! when the true clime nourishes you at last, in what enchanting glory will you not flower!

Diotima to Hyperion

I had shut myself up indoors most of the time since you went away, dear Hyperion! Today I went out again.

In the sweet February air I gathered life, and I bring you what I gathered. It did me good even yet, the fresh warming of the sky; even yet I felt in sympathy with the new joy of the plant world, ever pure, ever the same, where all things grieve and rejoice again in their time.

Hyperion! O my Hyperion! then why do not we too walk the quiet paths of life? They are holy names, winter and spring and summer and autumn! yet we know them not. Is it not a sin to grieve in spring? Why do we, then?

Forgive me! Earth's children live through the sun alone; I live through you; I have other joys, so is it any wonder if I have other griefs? and must I grieve? must I?

Brave one! loved one! shall I wither while you shine? shall my heart grow weary when the joy of victory wakes in your every vein? Had I heard in times past that a Greek youth had risen to raise our good people out of their shame, to give them back the maternal Beauty from which they are sprung, how I should have started from the dream of childhood and thirsted for the image of one so precious! and now that he is there, now that he is mine, can I still weep? Oh, the silly girl! is it not true? is he not the glorious one, and is he not mine! O ye shadows of a blessed time! ye my beloved memories!

Yet it seems as if it was scarcely yesterday, that magical evening when the sacred stranger came to me for the first time, when, like a grieving genius, he shone into the shadows of the wood where the carefree maiden sat in the dream of youth—in the air of May he came, in the enchanting May air of Ionia, and it made him the more blooming, it waved his hair, opened his lips like flowers, dissolved sorrow in smiles, and O ye rays of heaven! how ye shone on me from those eyes, from those intoxicating springs where in the shadow of screening brows eternal life shimmers and wells!—

Merciful Gods! how beautiful he became with his gaze upon me! how the whole youth, grown a span taller, stood there in easy strength, save that his dear, modest arms dropped down as if they were nothing! and how, then, he looked up in rapture, as if I had flown into the sky and were no longer there, ah! how, aware of me again, his eye shone bright as Phoebus through the darkening tears and, smiling, he blushed with inborn grace to ask me, "Is it you? is it you indeed?"

And why did he come to me with thoughts so devout, so full of dear superstition? why did he first stand with bowed head, why was the divine youth so full of shyness and grief? His genius was too blessed to remain alone, and the world too poor to comprehend him. Oh, it was a dear image, woven of greatness and sorrow! But now it is otherwise! the sorrowing is over! He has found work to do, he is sick no longer!—

I was full of sighs when I began to write to you, my beloved! Now I am pure joy. To talk of you has been to grow happy. And mark! even so shall it remain. Farewell!

Hyperion to Diotima

We have managed to celebrate your birthday, beautiful being! before the uproar begins. It was a heavenly day. The lovely springtime wafted and shone from the East, conjured your name from us as it conjures the flowers from the trees, and all the blessed secrets of love took my breath away. My friend had never known of such a love as ours, and it was ravishing to see how attentive the proud man became and how his eye and his spirit glowed as they strove to apprehend your image, your being.

"Oh," he cried at last, "our Greece is well worth fighting for when it still bears such offspring!"

"Yes indeed, my Alabanda," said I; "then we go joyfully into battle, then a divine fire drives us on to do high deeds when our spirit is rejuvenated by the image of such natures, then we run for no petty goal, then we are not concerned for this thing and that thing, do not tinker with outsides, unheeding the spirit, nor drink the wine for the cup's sake; then we will not rest, Alabanda, until the ecstasy of the Genius is a secret no longer, when all eyes are transformed into triumphal arches from which man's spirit, long absent, shines forth out of error and sufferings and greets the paternal ether in the joy of victory.—Ha! let no one think to know our people, as they are to be, from their flag alone; everything must be rejuvenated, everything be changed from the ground up; pleasure must be full of seriousness, and all work gleeful! nothing, not even the least and most commonplace of things, must be without spirit and the gods! Love and hate and every tone from us must make the commoner world wonder, not a single moment must ever dare to remind us of the flat past!"

Hyperion to Diotima

The volcano is erupting. The Turks are besieged in Coron and Modon and we are pushing on against the Peloponnesus with our mountaineers.

Now all depression is ended, Diotima, and my spirit is firmer and swifter since I am occupied with vital work and lo! I now even have a daily schedule.

I begin with the sun. I go out to where my troops are lying in the shadow of the woods and greet the thousand clear eyes that now open to me with wild affection. An awakening army! I know of nothing like it and all the life of towns and villages is like a swarm of bees in comparison.

Man cannot hide it from himself: once he was happy,

like the stag in the forest, and even now, after untold years, there rises in us a longing for the days of the primal world, when he roved over the earth like a god, before I know not what tamed man, and, instead of walls and dead wood, the soul of the World, sacred Air, still wrapped him in its universal presence.

Diotima! I am often filled with wonder when I go about among my carefree men and one after another stands up as if sprung from the earth and stretches himself toward the dawn, and among the martial groups the crackling flame rises, where the mother sits with the freezing infant, where the restoring dish is cooking, while the horses, sniffing the day, snort and whinny, and the wood resounds with shattering military music and everywhere glitters and rings with weapons—but these are words, and the unique pleasure of such a life cannot be told.

Then my troop gathers eagerly around me, and it is wonderful how even the oldest and most recalcitrant respect me, for all my youth. We become more and more intimate, and many a one of them tells me what his life has been and my heart often swells with their so various fates. Then I begin to speak of better days, and their eyes open wide and shine when they think of the covenant that will unite us, and the proud image of the free state that is soon to be looms before them.

All for each and each for all! There is a joyous spirit in the words, and always it catches up my men too, like a divine decree. O Diotima! to see how their stubborn natures are softened by hopes and all their pulses beat more strongly, and the gloom-clouded brow is smoothed and cleared by planning! to stand there in a sphere of men, surrounded by faith and joy—that is more, far more, than to behold earth and sky and sea in all their glory.

Then I drill them in weapons and marching until toward noon. The happy mood makes them eager pupils, as it makes me a teacher. Now they stand close together in the Macedonian phalanx, moving only their arms; now like rays they fly in different directions to more hazardous combat in separate squads, where their flexible strength changes with every position and each is his own general, then assemble again in a place of safety—and always, wherever they go or stand in this sort of war dance, before their eyes and mine floats the image of the tyrant's cohorts and the field of real battle.

Then, when the sun shines hotter, we hold council deep in the wood, and it is a joy thus in quiet thought to determine our great future. We strip chance of its power, we master destiny. We let resistance arise as suits our purpose, we lure the enemy into actions for which we are prepared. Or we bide our time and appear to be afraid and let him come nearer until he exposes his head to our blow, or we utterly disconcert him with our speed, and that is my cure-all. But the more experienced physicians do not hold with such a panacea.

After that, how well I feel in the evening, with my Alabanda, when we rove for pleasure around the sun-red hills on our spirited horses, and on the summits where we linger the wind plays in the manes of our mounts and the soothing rustle mingles with our talk, while we gaze into the distances of Sparta, which are the prize for which we shall fight! and then when we have returned and sit together in the pleasant cool of night, and the winecup is sweet in our nostrils and the moon's rays light our frugal meal, and amid our smiling silence the history of the men of old rises like a cloud from the soil that bears us, how blissful it is in such moments to grasp each other's hands!

Then perhaps Alabanda speaks of many another whom the ennui of this century torments, of so many a strangely crooked course that life takes, now that its straight path has been blocked, and then I think, too, of my Adamas, with his journeyings, his strange longing for the innermost parts of Asia—"These are but stopgaps, dear old man," I would fain cry to him then, "come! and build your world! with us! for our world is yours, too."

And yours, too, Diotima, for it is copied after you. O you, with your Elysian quiet, could we but create that which you are!

Hyperion to Diotima

We have now won three battles in succession—small ones, to be sure, but in them the combatants collided like thunderbolts and all was one consuming flame. Navarin is ours, and we are now before the fortress of Mistra, that remnant of ancient Sparta. And the flag that I wrested from an Albanian horde, I have planted on a ruin that lies before the city, and in my joy have thrown my Turkish turban into the Eurotas and since then wear the Greek casque.

And now would that I could see you, O maiden! that I could see you and take your hands and press them to my heart, whose joy will soon perhaps be too great! soon! in a week perhaps the old, noble land will be set free, the sacred Peloponnesus.

Then, O precious one, teach me to be pious! then teach my overflowing heart a prayer! I should be silent, for what have I done? and if I had done anything worth speaking of, how much is nonetheless left to do! But how can I help it if my thought is swifter than time? I wish so much that it were the other way around, that time and the deed overtook the thought, that winged victory outstripped the hope itself.

My Alabanda blooms like a bridegroom. From his every look the coming world smiles at me, and with that I still quiet my impatience more or less.

Diotima! I would not change this budding happiness for the most beautiful life that was ever lived in ancient Greece, and the smallest of our victories is dearer to me than Marathon and Thermopylae and Plataea. Is it not true? is not life recovering health more cherished than the pure life that has not yet known sickness? Not until youth is gone do we love it, not until what has been lost returns does it rejoice all the depths of the soul.

My tent is pitched beside the Eurotas, and when I wake up after midnight the ancient River God roars past ex-

horting me, and, smiling, I pick the flowers on the bank
and throw them into his shining waves and say to him:
"Take it as a sign, thou lonely one! Soon the old life
will bloom around thee again."

Diotima to Hyperion

I have received the letters, my Hyperion, that you have
written me along your way. You move me powerfully by
all that you say, and in the midst of my love I often
shudder to see the gentle youth who wept at my feet transformed into this robust being.

Will you not forget all that you have learned of love?

But change as you will! I follow you. I believe that if
you could hate me, I, too, should even come to feel as
you felt, would make an effort to hate you, and so our
souls would remain alike—and this that I say is no ex-
aggeration, Hyperion.

I, too, am wholly different from what I was. I have lost
my serene view of the world and my free delight in everything that has life. Only the field of the stars still draws
my eyes. On the other hand, I think all the more fondly
of the great spirits of the past and how they ended on
earth, and the noble women of Sparta have won my heart.
With all this, I do not forget the new champions, the
strong whose hour has come, I often hear their shouts of
victory through the Peloponnesus roar nearer and nearer to
me, I often see them surging down like a cataract through
the woods of Epidaurus, and their weapons glitter far
off in the sunlight that guides them on like a herald, O
my Hyperion! and you come swiftly across to Calaurea
and greet the quiet woods of our love, greet me, and then
fly back to your work;—and do you think I fear for the
outcome? Dearest! often I am close to being troubled,
but my nobler thoughts are like flames and hold off the
chill.—

Farewell! Accomplish what the spirit bids you! and
let not the war go on too long, for peace's sake, Hyperion,

for the sake of the beautiful, new, golden peace, when, as you said, the laws of Nature will yet be written in our statute book, and when life itself, when divine Nature, that can be written in no book, will dwell in the hearts of the community. Farewell.

Hyperion to Diotima

You should have calmed me, my Diotima! should have said that I must not go too fast, must extort victory from Fate by little and little, as what they owe is wrung from impecunious debtors. O maiden! to stand still is worse than anything. My blood dries up in my veins, I so thirst to go forward, and must stand here idle, laying siege day in and day out. Our men want to storm, but that would heat their excited spirits to frenzy, and alas! then for our hopes, if ever savagery erupts and bursts the bonds of discipline and love.

I do not know, it can be but a few days longer before Mistra must surrender, but I wish we were farther forward. Here in the camp I feel as if I were in the atmosphere of a brewing storm. I am impatient, and my men are not as I would have them. There is a recklessness among them that is terrifying.

But I am stupid to make so much of my state of mind. Yes, a little concern is a cheap price to pay for making ancient Lacedaemon ours.

Hyperion to Diotima

It is over, Diotima! our men have plundered, murdered, indiscriminately, even our brothers were killed, the innocent Greeks in Mistra, or they wander helplessly about, their woe-begone, dead countenances calling Heaven and Earth to wreak vengeance on the barbarians, whose leader I was.

Now indeed I can go forth and preach my good cause. Oh now indeed all hearts will fly to me!

How cleverly I went about it! How well I knew my men! Yes! it was indeed a remarkable undertaking, to establish my Elysium with the help of a robber band!

No! by sacred Nemesis! I have got what I deserved, and I will bear it too, bear it until the pain destroys my last consciousness.

Do you think I am raving? I have an honorable wound, which one of my faithful followers gave me while I was trying to avert the horror. If I were raving, I would tear the bandage from it, and then my blood would run where it should—into this sorrowing soil.

This sorrowing soil! whose nakedness I sought to clothe with sacred groves! this soil which I sought to adorn with all the flowers of Greek life!

Oh, it would have been beautiful, my Diotima!

Do you tell me I have lost faith? Dear girl! the evil is too great. Bands of madmen are bursting in on every side; rapacity rages like the plague in Morea, and he who does not also take the sword is hunted down and slain, and withal the maniacs say they are fighting for our freedom. Others of these wild men are paid by the Sultan and do the same things.

I have just heard that our dishonored army is now scattered. The cowards encountered a troop of Albanians near Tripolissa, only half as many as themselves. But since there was nothing to plunder, the wretches all ran away. Only the Russians who risked this campaign with us, forty brave men, put up a resistance, and they all found death.

So now I am again alone with my Alabanda, as before. Ever since he saw me fall and bleed in Mistra, that true-hearted friend has forgotten everything else—his hopes, his longing for victory, his despair. He who in his fury came down upon the plunderers like an avenging god, he led me out of the melee so gently, and his tears wet my clothes. He stayed with me, too, in the hut where I have lain since then, and only now am I glad that he did so. For had he gone on, he would now be lying in the dust before Tripolissa.

What is to follow I know not. Fate casts me adrift in

uncertainty, and I have deserved it; my own feeling of shame banishes me from you, and who knows for how long?

Ah! I promised you a Greece, and instead you receive only a threnody. Be your own consolation!

Hyperion to Diotima

I can scarcely bring myself to speak.

To be sure, men delight in speaking, they chatter away like the birds, so long as the world breathes upon them like the air of May; but between noon and evening that can change, and what is lost in the end?

Believe me, and consider that I say it to you from the depths of my soul: speech is a great superfluity. The best is ever for itself, and rests in its own depth like the pearl at the bottom of the sea.—But what I really wanted to write to you is this: because the painting needs its frame and man his daily work, I am now going to take service for a time in the Russian fleet; for I have nothing more to do with the Greeks.

O dear girl! It has grown very dark about me!

Hyperion to Diotima

I have hesitated, I have struggled. But now at last it must be.

I see what is necessary. And since I see it, it shall come to pass. Do not misunderstand me! do not condemn me! I must advise you to give me up, my Diotima.

I am nothing more for you, lovely being! This heart has dried up toward you, and my eyes no more see what has life. Oh, my lips have withered; the sweet breath of love no longer wells up in my breast.

One day has taken all my youth from me; beside the

Eurotas my life wept itself weary, ah! beside the Eurotas which, in irreparable dishonor, goes mourning with its every wave past Lacedaemon's ruins. There, there did Fate mow down my harvest.—Am I to have your love as an alms?—I am as utterly nothing, as inglorious, as the most wretched serf. I am banished, cursed, like a common rebel, and many a Greek in Morea will hereafter narrate our heroic deeds to his children's children as a tale of robbers.

And, ah! I have long kept one thing from you. My father has solemnly disowned me, banished me irrevocably from the home of my youth, he will never see me again, either in this life or the next, as he puts it. So reads the answer to the letter in which I wrote to him of my undertaking.

But let not pity, now or ever, lead you astray. Believe me, there is one joy left for us everywhere. True grief inspires. He who steps on his misery stands higher. And it is glorious that only in suffering do we truly feel freedom of soul. Freedom! if any understand the word—it is a deep word, Diotima. I am so inwardly assailed, so extraordinarily hurt, I am without hope, without a goal, utterly dishonored, and yet there is a power in me, something indomitable, that sets my frame sweetly trembling whenever it awakes in me.

And I still have my Alabanda. He has as little to gain as I have. I can keep him for myself without injuring him. Ah! the kingly youth would have deserved a better lot. He has become so gentle and so quiet. It often comes near to breaking my heart. But each of us sustains the other. We do not talk together; what should we say? but there is a blessing in many little affectionate services that we render each other.

There he sleeps, smiling resignedly, in all our misfortune. The good soul! he does not know what I am doing. He would not tolerate it. "You must write to Diotima," he ordered me, "and tell her to be ready soon to fly with you to a more endurable country." But he does not know that a heart that has learned to despair like his and like mine is nothing more for its beloved. No! no! you would forever find no peace with Hyperion, you could not but be unfaithful, and that I shall spare you.

And so farewell, sweet maid! farewell! Would that I could say to you: "Go here, go there; there the springs of life murmur." Would that I could show you a freer country, a country filled with beauty and soul, and say: "Escape thither." But, O Heaven! if I could do that, I should be other than I am, and then I should not need to take my leave—take leave? Ah, I know not what I am doing. I thought that I was so self-possessed, so cool-headed. Now my brain reels, my heart tosses like an impatient sick man. Woe to me! I am destroying my last happiness. But it must be, and mortal nature's "Alas!" is unavailing here. I owe it to you, and, besides that, I was born to be homeless and without a resting place. O Earth! O ye Stars! shall I find nowhere to abide, even to the end?

Could I but once return to your arms, no matter where! Eyes clear as the ether! could I but once again find myself in you! hang on those lips of yours, O lovable, inexpressible one! and drink down your ravishing, blessed sweet life—but listen not to this! I implore you, heed it not! If you listened, I should say I am a seducer. You know me, you understand me. You recognize what deep respect you pay me, if you do not pity me, do not listen to me.

I have strength for no more, no more am I permitted —how should the priest live when his God is no more? O Genius of my people! O Soul of Greece! I must go down, to seek you in the realm of the dead.

Hyperion to Diotima

I have waited long, I will confess to you, I have hoped anxiously for a parting word from your heart, but you are silent. That, too, is a language of your beautiful soul, Diotima.

Is it not true that the more sacred harmonies do not

therefore cease? is it not true, Diotima, that even when the soft moonlight of love sets, the higher stars of its heaven still shine on? Oh, that is indeed my last joy, that we are inseparable, even if no sound returns to me from you, no shadow of our fair young days.

I gaze out to the sunset-red sea, I stretch my arms toward the far place where you live, and my soul is warmed once again by all the joys of love and youth.

O Earth! my cradle! all bliss and all sorrow is in our leave-taking from thee!

Ye dear Ionian islands! and thou, my Calaurea, and thou, my Tina, ye are all before my eyes, distant though ye be, and my spirit flies with the breeze over the moving waters; and ye that loom dimly over there, ye shores of Teos and Ephesus, where once I walked with Alabanda in the days of hope, ye appear to me again as in that time, and I would fain sail across to the mainland and kiss that soil and warm it at my breast and stammer out all sweet words of farewell to the silent Earth, before I wing up into freedom.

Alas, alas, that things are not now in better case among mankind! were it otherwise, I would gladly remain upon this goodly star. But I can forego this globe of the Earth, and that is more than all that it can give.

"Let us bear slavery, O child, in the light of the Sun," said her mother to Polyxena, and her love of life could find no more beautiful expression. But it is the light of the Sun that exhorts me not to bear slavery, that will not let me remain upon the degraded Earth, and his holy rays draw me on, like paths that lead home.

Long since has the majesty of the soul that is outside of Fate been more present to me than anything else; I have often lived within myself in glorious solitude; I have grown used to shaking off outside things like flakes of snow; why, then, should I be afraid to seek so-called death? have I not freed myself a thousand times in thought? why should I hesitate to do it once in reality? Are we like thralls, then, bound to the soil that we plow? are we like barnyard fowls, which dare not run out of the courtyard because they are fed there?

We are like young eagles whose father drives them out

of the nest that they may seek their prey in the high ether.

Tomorrow our fleet goes into action, and the fight will be hot enough. I look on this battle as a bath that will wash the dust from me; and I shall doubtless find what I wish for; wishes like mine are easily granted, and on the spot. And so I should have gained something after all from my campaign, and behold! no effort that man makes is wholly in vain.

Devout soul! I would fain say, "Think of me when you come upon my grave." But they will doubtless throw me into the sea, and I am content to have my remains sink down where the springs and all the rivers that I loved gather together, and where the storm cloud arises to drench the mountains and the valleys that I loved. And we? O Diotima! Diotima! when shall we see each other once again?

It is impossible, and my inmost life rebels if I try to think that we are lost to each other. I would wander among the stars for millenniums, clothe myself in all forms, in all the languages of life, that I might meet you once again. But I think that what is alike is soon united.

Great soul! you will be able to reconcile yourself to this parting, and so let me be off on my journey! Greet your mother! greet Notara and our other friends!

And greet the trees where I found you for the first time and the joyous brooks where we walked and the lovely gardens of Angele, and, dear one, let my image be before you then. Farewell.

BOOK TWO

Hyperion to Bellarmin

I was in a lovely dream when I copied out for you the letters that I once exchanged. Now I write to you again, my Bellarmin! and lead you yet further down, down into the deepest depth of my sorrow; and then, you last of my loves! come out with me again, to the place where a new day shines upon us.

The battle of which I had written to Diotima began. The Turkish ships had withdrawn into the strait between the island of Chios and the Asiatic coast, and had taken up a position along the mainland near Cheshme. My admiral left the line with his ship, on which I was, and began the prelude with the first Turkish ship. The enraged pair were heated to frenzy at the very first attack, it was an intoxication of revenge, a terrible melee. The ships were soon fast together by their rigging; the furious fight was ever at closer quarters.

A profound sense of life still pervaded me. I felt warm and well in every limb. My spirit, like one taking tender leave, was aware of itself for the last time in all its senses. And now, filled with hot disgust at knowing nothing better than to let myself be slaughtered in a crush of barbarians, I rushed on, with tears of rage in my eyes, to where certain death awaited me. I had not far to seek for the enemy, and it was not many minutes before, of the Russians who were fighting beside me, not even one was left.

I stood there alone, filled with pride, and flung my life down before the barbarians like a beggar's penny; but they would have none of me. They looked at me as at a man whom one is afraid to offend, and Fate seemed to feel consideration for me in my despair.

In desperate self-defense, one of them at last aimed a blow at me, striking me so that I fell. After that I knew nothing, until I came to my senses again in Paros, whither I had been brought by ship.

From the servant who carried me out of the battle I later heard that the two ships that had begun the fight had blown up the moment after he and the surgeon had taken me off in a boat. The Russians had thrown fire into the Turkish ship; and since theirs was fast to the other, it had burned too.

How this terrible battle ended, you know. "Thus one poison wreaks vengeance upon the other," I cried, when I learned that the Russians had burned the entire Turkish fleet—"thus do tyrants exterminate themselves."

Hyperion to Bellarmin

Six days after the battle I lay in a tortured sleep that resembled death. My life was like a night interrupted by pains as it were by darting lightning. My first returning consciousness was of Alabanda. He had not—so I learned —stirred from my side for an instant, had taken care of me almost single-handed, with incredible assiduity, with a thousand tender, homely services of which he would otherwise never in his life have thought, and he had been heard to cry, on his knees beside my bed: "O live, my loved one, that I may live!"

It was a happy awakening, Bellarmin! when my eyes opened to the light again, and the glorious youth stood before me with tears of emotion at our reunion.

I held out my hand, and, proud as he was, he kissed it with all the rapture of love. "He lives," he cried, "O Nature, O kindly, all-healing savior! thou dost not, wilt

not forsake thy wretched pair, thy wanderers without a
country. O Hyperion! never will I forget seeing your ship
go up in fire before my eyes and, thundering, carry the
sailors with it in raging flame, and among the few who
were saved there was no Hyperion. I was out of my mind,
and the fierce clamor of battle did not quiet me. But I
soon heard news of you and flew after you as soon as
we had finished with the enemy."—

And how he watched over me now! with what loving
caution he kept me imprisoned in the magic circle of his
kind services! how, without a word, he taught me by his
great quietude to understand the free course of the world
without envy and like a man!

O ye sons of the Sun! ye freer souls! much has been
lost in this Alabanda. I sought in vain, in vain I prayed
to Life; since he is gone, such a Roman nature I have
never found. Untroubled, profoundly understanding,
brave, noble Alabanda! where is there a man if he was
not one? And when he was friendly and simple, it was as
when the light of evening plays through the darkness of
the majestic oak and its leaves drip with the rainstorm of
the day.

Hyperion to Bellarmin

It was in the beautiful days of autumn that, half recovered from my wound, I made my way to the window
again for the first time. I returned to life with calmer senses
and my soul had grown more attentive. The air of
heaven breathed its most delicate magic upon me, the
serene sunbeams poured down as mildly as a rain of
flowers. There was a great, quiet, tender spirit in the season; and among the rustling twigs the peace of completion,
the bliss of maturity surrounded me like the renewed
youth for which the Ancients hoped in their Elysium.

It had been long since I had enjoyed it in purity of
soul, this childlike love of the world; now my eyes opened
with all the joy of recognition and blessed Nature had

remained unchanged in her beauty. My tears flowed before her like an atoning sacrifice, and a heart renewed rose tremblingly from my old discontent. "O holy world of plants!" I cried, "we struggle and take thought, and yet have thee! with our mortal powers we strive to cultivate the Beautiful, yet it grows light-heartedly beside us! Is it not so, Alabanda? men are made to provide for their necessities, all else is freely given. And yet—I cannot forget how much more I wanted."

"Let it suffice you, dear one, that you exist," cried Alabanda, "and let grieving no longer hinder what is quietly at work within you."

"Yes, I will rest," said I. "Oh, I will tear up all those projects, all those claims, like notes of hand. I will keep myself pure, as an artist keeps himself, thee will I love, innocent Life, Life of the grove and the spring! thee will I honor, O light of the Sun! by thee will I calm myself, beautiful Ether, which givest life to the stars and yet here breathest about these trees and here touchest us in the depths of our hearts! O willfulness of men! I have bowed my neck like a beggar, and the Gods of Nature watched me in silence with all their gifts!—Do you smile, Alabanda? Oh how often, in our earliest days, did you smile so when your lad chattered to you in the intoxicated pride of youth, the while you stood like a quiet temple pillar amid the rubble of the world and could not but suffer the wild tendrils of my love to grow about you—see what a blindfold falls from my eyes, and the old golden days are here and live again!"

"Ah!" he cried, "the earnestness that was ours, and the joy of life!"

"When we hunted in the forest," I cried, "when we bathed in the sea, when we sang and drank, and through the laurel shade the sun and the wine and our eyes and our lips were bright—that was a life without equal and our spirit illuminated our youthful happiness like a shining heaven." "And therefore neither of us can abandon the other," said Alabanda.

"Oh, I have a heavy confession to make to you," said I. "Will you believe that I wanted to go away? from you! that I sought my death by main strength? was that not

heartless? madness? ah, and my Diotima! she must leave
me, I wrote to her, and after that another letter, the evening before the battle—" "and you wrote in it," he cried,
"that you would seek your end in the battle? O Hyperion!
But she cannot yet have received that last letter. You must
write to her, quickly, that you are still alive."

"Best Alabanda!" I cried. "You comfort me indeed!
I will write at once and send my servant off with it.
Oh, I will offer him all that I have to hurry and reach
Calaurea while it is still time."—

"And the other letter, in which you wrote of renunciation—the good soul will easily understand and forgive
you for that," he added.

"Does she forgive?" I cried; "O all ye hopes! yes! if I
could still be happy with that angel!"

"You will still be happy," cried Alabanda; "the most
beautiful age of life is yet left to you. The youth is a
hero, the man a god, if he can live to see it."

A wondrous light dawned in my soul as he spoke.

The tops of the trees stirred softly; like flowers from
the dark ground, stars sprouted from the womb of night
and the springtime of the heavens shone on me in holy
joy.

Hyperion to Bellarmin

A few minutes later, just as I was about to write to
Diotima, Alabanda came joyfully back into the room. "A
letter, Hyperion!" he cried; I gave a start and flew to it.

"How long," wrote Diotima, "I had to live without a
sign from you! You wrote me about the fatal day at Mistra,
and I answered speedily; but everything would indicate
that you did not receive my letter. Immediately afterward you wrote to me again, briefly and gloomily, and
said you were of a mind to join the Russian fleet; I
answered again; but that letter did not reach you either;
now I, too, waited in vain, from May to the end of

summer, until some days ago the letter arrived which tells me I should renounce you, beloved!

"You relied on me, had enough trust in me to believe that your letter could not offend me. That made me heartily glad, even in my distress.

"Unhappy, lofty spirit! I have understood you only too well. Oh, it is so completely natural that you will not love, because your greater wishes are dying a lingering death. Must you not scorn food when you are perishing of thirst?

"I soon understood: I could not be all to you. Could I loose the bonds of mortality for you? could I quiet the flame in your breast, that flame for which no spring flows and no vine bears grapes? could I offer you the joys of a world in a scallop shell?

"That is what you want. That is what you need, and you cannot do otherwise. The unbounded impotence of your contemporaries has robbed you of your life.

"He who, like you, has been hurt to the depths of his soul can no longer find rest in an individual joy, he who, like you, has felt nothingness in all its vapidity finds exhilaration only in the highest spirit, he who has experienced death as you did recovers only among the gods.

"They are fortunate—all those who do not understand you! He who understands you must share in your greatness and in your despair.

"I found you as you are. Life's first curiosity impelled me toward that wonderful being. Your tender soul drew me inexpressibly on, with the fearlessness of a child I played about your dangerous flame.—The beautiful joys of our love softened you; but only, wicked man! to make you the more savage. They soothed, they solaced me, too, they made me forget that you were essentially inconsolable, and that I, too, was not far from becoming so ever since I had looked into your beloved heart.

"In Athens, beside the ruins of the Olympieion, it came over me again. In carefree hours, it is true, I had been thinking: This youth's sorrow is not perhaps so deep and inexorable. It is so seldom that a man, at his first step into life, has so suddenly, so minutely, so quickly, so deeply felt the whole inevitable course of his time, and

that this feeling is so ineradicably fixed in him because
he is not rugged enough to cast it out and not weak
enough to weep it away—that, my dear one, is so unusual that we think it almost out of the course of Nature.

"Now, in the rubble of serene Athens, it came home
to me all too grievously: the leaf has been turned, the
dead now walk the earth and the living, the divine men,
are under it, now I saw it all too literally and all too
really written on your face, now I admitted that you were
eternally right. But at the same moment I saw you greater.
A being filled with secret strength, filled with a deep, un-
developed significance, a youth uniquely promising—thus
you appeared to me. 'He to whom Destiny speaks so
loudly has the right to speak yet more loudly to Destiny,'
I told myself; 'the more unfathomably he suffers, the more
unfathomably strong he is.' From you, from you alone,
I hoped for all restoration. I saw you traveling. I saw
you working. Oh, the transformation! Established by you,
the grove of Academe spread green again over listening
pupils, and the plane tree of the Ilissus heard sacred conversations, as of old.

"In your school the genius of our youths soon acquired
the seriousness of the Ancients, its transitory games became more nearly immortal, for it felt ashamed, deemed
its butterfly flight a prison.—

"To manage a horse would have sufficed one of them;
now he is a general. Only too contentedly would another
have sung an idle song; now he is an artist. For you had
revealed the powers of the heroes, the powers of the world
to them in open battle; you had given them the riddles of
your heart to solve; so the youths learned to bring together great things, learned to understand the living play
of Nature, and forgot jesting.—Hyperion! Hyperion!
did you not make me, immature as I was, a Muse? So it
was, too, with the others.

"Ah! now men, born to companionship, did not so
easily forsake one another; no longer did they wander in
mutual confusion, like sand in the desert storm, nor did
youth and age mock each other, nor did the stranger want
for a hospitable host, and fellow countrymen no longer
stood aside, and lovers no longer tired of each other; at

thy springs, Nature, they refreshed themselves, ah! at the
sacred joys that pour secretly from thy depths and renew the spirit; and the gods restored to the souls of men
the joy without which they wither away; the heart-
sustaining gods were guardians of every bond of friendship. For you, Hyperion! had healed the eyes of your
Greeks so that they saw the living, you had kindled the
enthusiasm that slept in them like fire in wood so that
they felt the still, never-failing enthusiasm of Nature and
of her pure children. Ah! now men no longer took the
beautiful world as the uninitiated take the artist's poem
when they praise the words of it and look for profit in
them. O living Nature, thou didst become a magical example to the Greeks, and, fired by the happiness of the
ever-young gods, all the activities of men were, as of
old, a festival; and more beautiful than martial music,
Helios' light escorted the young heroes to high deeds.

"Enough! enough! it was my most beautiful dream, my
first and my last. You are too proud any longer to concern yourself with this villainous race. And you are right.
You led them to freedom, and they thought of robbery.
You led them victoriously into their ancient Lacedaemon,
and these monsters fall to plundering and you are cursed
by your father, great son! and no wilderness, no cave is
safe enough for you on this Greek soil that you revered
as a sacred shrine, that you loved more than you loved me.

"O my Hyperion! I am no longer the gentle maiden,
since I have learned all this. Indignation bears me upward
so that I can hardly see down to the Earth, and my offended heart trembles incessantly.

"We will part. You are right. And I want no children;
for I will not bestow them on this world of slaves, and
besides, the poor plants would wither away before my
eyes in this drought.

"Farewell, dear youth! go wherever you think it worth
going to yield up your soul. The world must yet have one
battlefield, some place of sacrifice, where you can free
yourself. It would be a shame if all these goodly powers
but vanished like a dream. But however you find your
end, you return to the gods, return into the sacred, free,

youthful life of Nature, whence you came, and that is your desire as it is mine."

So she wrote to me. I was stricken to the marrow, filled with terror and joy, but I tried to control myself and find words in which to answer.

"You assent, Diotima?" I wrote, "you approve of my renunciation? you could understand it?—Loyal soul! you could reconcile yourself to it? could reconcile yourself even to my dark wanderings, in your heavenly patience? you submitted, eclipsed yourself for love, happy child of Nature? became like me and by your concurrence sanctified my grief? Beautiful heroine! what crown did you not earn?

"But now let there be enough of grieving, O loved one! You have followed me into my darkness, now come! and let me follow you to your light, let us return to your graces, beautiful heart! oh, let me look upon your calm once again, blessed nature! let me lull my discontent to sleep forever before you, image of peace!

"Is it not true, dear one! it is not too late for me to return even now? and you will take me back and can love me again, as before? is it not true that the happiness of past days is not lost to us?

"I have behaved unconscionably. I have dealt most ungratefully with Mother Earth; my blood and all the gifts of love that she gave me, I have thrown away like the base wage of a serf, and ah! how many thousand times more ungrateful have I been to you, O sacred maiden! who once received me into her peace, me, a shy, lacerated being from whose sorely oppressed heart scarcely a glimmer of youth stole forth, as here and there a grass blade steals up from trodden paths. Had you not called me to life? was I not yours? then how could I—oh, you know not yet, I hope, it has not yet reached your hands, the unhappy letter that I wrote to you before the last battle? I wanted to die then, Diotima, and I thought thus to perform a sacred act. But how can that be sacred which parts lovers? how can that be sacred which destroys the innocent happiness of our lives?—O Diotima! O life born in beauty! now I have become all the more like you in what is most uniquely yourself, I have at last learned to value, I have learned to guard, what is good and intrinsic on earth. Oh, even if I could land up there, on the shining islands of the sky, should I find more than I find in Diotima?

"Hear me now, beloved!

"In Greece I can remain no longer. That you know. When he dismissed me my father sent me enough out of what he could spare to enable us to flee to some blessed valley in the Alps or the Pyrenees and there to buy a pleasant house and with it as much green ground as life's golden mean requires.

"If you are willing, I will come at once and conduct you and your mother with a loyal arm, we will kiss the shore of Calaurea and dry our tears and hasten across the Isthmus to the Adriatic Sea, where a safe ship will take us farther.

"Oh come! in the depths of the mountain world the secret of our hearts will rest like the precious stone in the mine; in the bosom of woods that tower to the sky we shall be as among the pillars of the inmost temple, where the godless draw not near; and we shall sit by the spring, and behold our world in it—sky and house and garden and ourselves. On a clear night we shall often wander in our orchard's shade and listen for the loving god in us, while the plant raises its bowed head from its midday sleep, and the still life of your flowers is refreshed when they bathe their tender arms in the dew and the night air breathes its penetrating coolness around them, and above us the meadow of the sky blooms with all its twinkling flowers, and to one side the moon behind westerly clouds shyly imitates the setting of the youthful sun as if for love of him—and then in the morning when our valley is like a riverbed filled with warm light, and the golden stream runs silently through our trees and flows around our house and makes the lovely room that is your handiwork more beautiful for you, and you move through its sunny brightness and, in your grace, bless the day for me, beloved! then, as we thus celebrate the delight of morning, when the busy life of Earth is kindled before our eyes like a burnt sacrifice and we go forth to our day's work, to cast our share, too, into the rising flame, will you not say then, 'We are happy, we are again like the ancient priests of Nature, who, sacred and free, were already pious before ever a temple stood'?

"Have I said enough? now decide my fate, dear maid, and soon!—It is fortunate that I am still half an invalid, as I have been since the last battle, and that I have not yet been released from service; otherwise I could not remain here, I could not but go myself, ask you myself, and that would not be right, for it would be to besiege you.—

"Ah, Diotima! anxious, foolish thoughts assail my heart, and yet—I cannot think that this hope, too, will founder.

"Are you perhaps become too great to return now to earthly happiness? does the mighty flame of spirit that was kindled at your sorrow, does it perhaps consume all that is mortal in you?

"I know well that he who lightly quarrels with the world is reconciled with it even more lightly. But you, who have the quiet of a child, you, once so happy in your high humility, Diotima! who shall reconcile you when your quarrel is with destiny?

"Dear life! is there then no more power of healing for you in me? of all the notes of the heart, does none any longer call you back to the life of men, where once you lingered so beautifully in descended flight? oh, come! oh, remain in this twilight! This shadow-land is surely love's element, only here does the quiet dew of melancholy run from the heaven of your eyes.

"And do you no longer remember our golden days, those enchanting, divinely melodious days? do they not rustle to you from all the groves of Calaurea?

"And see! so much has perished in me, and I have few hopes left. Your image with its heavenly awareness—that I still have, like a household god saved from the conflagration. Our life, ours, is still inviolate in me. Should I now arise and bury this too? Shall I go forth, with no rest and no goal, from one homelessness to another? Is it for this that I learned to love?

"No, no! you my first and my last! You were mine, mine you shall remain."

Hyperion to Bellarmin

I was sitting with Alabanda on a hill near where we were staying, in the kindly warmth of the sun, and around us the wind played with fallen leaves. The countryside was quiet; save that, now and again, a tree felled by the farmer crashed far away in the woods and, close by, the intermittent rain-fed stream murmured down to the peaceful sea.

I was almost carefree; I hoped to see my Diotima soon now, soon now to live with her in quiet happiness. Alabanda had talked me out of all my doubts; he was so certain of it himself. He, too, was serene; but in another sense. The future had no more power over him. Oh, I did not know it: he was at the end of his joys; with all his claims on the world, all his conquering nature, he saw himself useless, ineffectual, and alone, and he accepted it as if he had lost some game played but to while away the time.

A messenger arrived. He brought us the discharge from military service for which we had both petitioned the command of the Russian fleet because there was nothing left for us to do that seemed worth the effort. I could now leave Paros whenever I pleased. And I was now well enough to travel. I did not want to wait for Diotima's answer, I wanted to be off to her; it was as if a god were driving me to Calaurea. When Alabanda heard me say this, his color changed and he looked at me sorrowfully. "Is it so easy for my Hyperion," he cried, "to forsake his Alabanda?"

"Forsake?" I said. "What do you mean?"

"Oh, you dreamers!" he cried. "Do you not see that we must part?"

"How should I see it?" I answered; "you have not said a word about it; and what I have seen in you now and again that seemed to point to a separation I took in good

part as a momentary mood, as coming from a heart too
full—"

"Oh, I know it well," he cried, "that divine game when
love in its wealth pretends to be in need, so that it can
shower its plenty on itself; and I would that it were thus
with me, good heart! but in this case I am in earnest!"

"In earnest?" I cried. "But why?"

"Why, my Hyperion?" he said gently. "Because I should
not wish to trouble your future happiness, because I cannot but fear to be close to Diotima. Believe me, it is
risky to live with lovers, and a heart with nothing to do,
as mine now is, can scarcely bear it."

"Ah, my good Alabanda," I said with a smile, "how
little you know yourself! You are not such a thing of wax,
and your steadfast soul is not so easily carried out of its
domain. For the first time in your life you give in to
groundless fancies. You played nurse for me here, and it
is plain to see how little your nature is suited to it. This
sitting about doing nothing has made you timorous—"

"There you are!" he cried, "that is it exactly. Living
with you and Diotima, should I be any more active? If
it were some other woman! but this Diotima! can I help
it? can I feel her with half my soul? she, who is so utterly
at one with herself, one divinely undivided life? Believe
me, it is childishness to undertake to see such a being
and not love her. You look at me as if you did not
know me, do you? But I have grown a stranger to myself
these last days, since her being has become so living a
presence in me."

"Oh, why cannot I give her to you?" I cried.

"Enough!" he said. "Do not try to console me, for here
there is no place for consolation, I am alone, alone, and
my life is running out like an hourglass."

"Great soul!" I cried, "must it come to this for you?"

"Accept what is!" he said. "I was already beginning
to wither when we found each other in Smyrna. Yes! in
the days when I was still a ship's boy and my spirit and
all my limbs were strong and swift on coarse food and
daring work! In those days, when in the clear air after
a stormy night I clung to the top of the mast under the
billowing flag and gazed after the seabird over the shining

deep, when in frequent battle our raging ships tore up the sea as the boar's tusk tears the earth and I stood at my captain's side clear-eyed—in those days I lived, oh, then I lived! And long after that, when the young Tiniote met me on the Smyrnean shore, with his earnestness, and his love, and my hardened soul was bedewed again by the youth's gaze and learned to love and to hold sacred all that is too good to be subdued, when I began a new life with him, and new, more spiritual powers germinated in me to make me better able to delight in the world and to struggle with it, then I hoped again—ah! and all that I hoped and had was inseparably linked with you; I took you to me, sought to drag you into my destiny by force, lost you, found you again, our friendship alone was my world, my value, my fame; now that is over too, forever, and my whole existence is in vain."

"But is that true?" I answered, sighing.

"True as the sun," he cried, "but let it be! Everything is provided for."

"What do you mean, my Alabanda?" said I.

"Let me tell you," he said. "I have never yet spoken to you fully about a certain matter. And then—it quiets both you and me a little when we talk of the past.

"Once long ago, helpless and desperate, I was wandering about the waterfront of Trieste. The privateer on which I was serving had been shipwrecked some years earlier, and I had barely managed to save myself, with a few others, on the shore near Seville. My captain was drowned and my life and my dripping garments were all that remained to me. I undressed and rested in the sunshine and dried my clothes on the bushes. Then I resumed my journey along the road to the city. Before I came to the gates, I saw people making merry in the gardens; I entered and sang a gay Greek song. I did not know a sad one. All the while I was hot with the shame and pain of exhibiting my misfortune in this way. I was an eighteen-year-old boy, wild and proud, and I hated like death to be the object of people's attention. 'Forgive me,' I said, when I had finished my song; 'I have just escaped from a shipwreck and at present know no better way to do the world a service than to sing to it.' I had said

this in such Spanish as I could muster. A man with a
fine face came up to me, gave me money, and, speaking
our language, said with a smile: 'There! buy yourself a
grindstone with that and learn to sharpen knives, and
you can resume your travels, but on dry land!' The advice pleased me. 'Sir! I will do just that,' I answered. All
the others rewarded me liberally too, and I left them and
did as the man had advised me, and so wandered for a
time through Spain and France.

"What I experienced during that time, how the thousand forms that servitude assumes intensified my love of
freedom and many a hard hour of need increased my
courage to live and sharpened my wits, I have often delighted in telling you.

"I practiced my innocent, wandering trade with pleasure,
but finally it was spoiled for me.

"People took it to be a mask, probably because I did
not look mean enough for such an occupation; they
imagined I was covertly engaged in some dangerous undertaking, and in fact I was twice arrested. All this decided
me to give it up, and with the little money I had earned
I set out to make my way back to the home from which
I had run away. I was soon in Trieste and about to start
down through Dalmatia. Just then the accumulated hard-
ships of my journey laid me low with an illness that made
my small capital vanish. Only half recovered, I was
wandering sadly along the waterfront at Trieste. Suddenly,
there stood the man who had once befriended me when
I was cast ashore at Seville. He was wonderfully glad to
see me, told me that he often thought of me, and asked
how things had gone with me meanwhile. I told him all.
'I see,' he cried, 'that it was no bad thing to send you to
the school of Fate for a while. You have learned endurance, now you shall go to work whenever you please.'

"The words, his tone, his handclasp, his manner, his
look, all went like some divine force to my inmost being,
which much suffering had now made even more inflam-
mable than before, and I surrendered.

"The man of whom I speak, Hyperion, was one of
those whom you saw with me in Smyrna. The very next
night he introduced me to the members of a solemn society.

A shudder ran through me as I entered the room and my companion, pointing to the earnest group of men, said: 'This is the League of Nemesis.' Intoxicated by the immense sphere of action that opened before me, I solemnly made over my blood and my soul to these men. Soon afterward the meeting was adjourned, to be reconvened in some other place years later, and each set out on the appointed path that he was to follow through the world. I was made an associate of those whom you found with me some years afterward in Smyrna.

"The constraint under which I lived often tortured me; then too, I saw little of the great accomplishments of the League and my longing for action found short commons. But all this was not enough to enable me to desert. My love for you finally led me away. I have often told you that I was as if without air and sun when you were absent; and I had no other choice: I must give up either you or my League. What I chose, you see.

"But every human act finds its punishment at last; only gods and children are not smitten by Nemesis.

"I put the divine right of the heart first. For my dear one's sake I broke my oath. Was not that right? must not the noblest longing be the freest?—My heart took me at my word; I gave it freedom, and you see it uses it.

"Once do homage to the Genius and he will heed no mortal hindrance thereafter, he will tear all the bonds of life in two for you.

"I broke my obligation for my friend's sake, I would break friendship for the sake of love. For Diotima's sake I would betray you, and finally kill Diotima and myself because, even so, we should not be one. But it shall stop here; if I must pay for what I did, I will do it freely; I choose my own judge; those whom I failed shall have me."

"Do you speak of your fellows in the League?" I cried; "O my Alabanda! do it not!"

"What can they take from me but my blood?" he answered. Then he gently clasped my hand. "Hyperion!" he cried, "my time has run out, and all that remains to me is a noble end. Leave me! do not make me less than I am, have faith in my word! I know as well as you do that I could still trump up some kind of an existence for myself, could, now that life's meal is eaten, still sit playing with the crumbs; but that is not for me; nor for you. Need I say more? Do I not speak to you from your own soul? I thirst for air, for coolness, Hyperion. My soul seethes over of itself and will no longer be confined to the old circle. Soon the beautiful days of winter will be here, when the dark earth is but the foil to the shining heavens—that would be the right time, then the isles of light glimmer the more hospitably!—You are amazed by what I say? Dearest one, all who are departing talk like drunken men and delight to behave as at a feast. When the tree begins to wither, do not all its leaves bear the red of morning?"

"Great soul," I cried, "must I bear to pity you?"

I sensed from his exaltation how deeply he was suffering. I had never felt such grief in my life. And yet, O Bellarmin, yet I felt the greatness of all joys, to hold such a godlike figure in my eyes and arms. "Yes! die," I cried, "die! Your heart is glorious enough, your life is ripe, like grapes in autumn. Go, perfected one! I would go with you, if there were no Diotima."

"Have I convinced you now?" answered Alabanda, "are these your words? how deep, how full of soul does all become when once my Hyperion comprehends it!" "He flatters," I cried, "to wheedle the unconsidered word from me a second time! good gods! to wrest leave from me for his journey to the tribunal of blood!"

"I do not flatter," he answered gravely, "I have a right to do what you would prevent, and no common right! Honor it!"

There was a fire in his eyes that struck me down like a divine command, and I felt ashamed to say another word in opposition to him.

"They will not," I thought meanwhile, "they cannot do it. It is too senseless to slaughter such a glorious life, like a sacrificial animal," and this conviction calmed me.

It was strangely profitable still to hear him the following night, when each of us had made ready for his separate journey and, just before daybreak, we had gone out again to be alone together once more.

"Do you know," he said, among other things, "why I have never thought anything but lightly of death? I feel a life in me which no god created and no mortal begot. I believe that our existence is from ourselves and that it is only of our own free pleasure that we are so intimately connected with all that is."

"I have never heard you say such a thing before," I replied.

"And what," he went on, "what would this world itself be, if it were not a harmony of free beings? if from the beginning the living did not work together, of their own free impulse, in one full-voiced life, how wooden would it not be? how cold? what heartless trumpery?"

"So it would be true here in the highest sense," I answered, "that without freedom all is dead."

"Yes, yes," he cried, "why! not a blade of grass sprouts up if it has not its own seed of life within it! And how much more in me! and therefore, dear lad, because I feel that I am free in the highest sense, that I have no beginning, therefore I believe that I shall have no end, that I am indestructible. If a potter's hand made me, he may smash his vessel whenever he pleases. But what lives must be unbegotten, must be of divine nature in its seed, raised above all force and all art, and therefore inviolable, eternal.

"Every man has his mysteries, dear Hyperion! his more secret thoughts; these were mine—ever since I have thought.

"What lives is ineradicable, remains free in its deepest form of servitude, remains one even if you split it to the base, remains unwounded even if you pierce it to the marrow and its being flies victorious from your hands.— But the morning wind freshens; our ships are awake. O my Hyperion! I have won through; I have had the strength to pronounce the death sentence on my heart and to divide you and me, beloved of my life! be tender to me now! spare me your leave-taking! let us be quick! come!—"

A chill ran through my every bone, as I heard him begin thus.

"Oh, by your loyalty, Alabanda!" I cried, prostrate before him, "must it be, must it be indeed? You shouted me down unfairly, you dragged me along in a frenzy.

Brother! you did not leave me sense enough even to ask: 'Where are you going?' "

"I may not name the place, dear heart!" he answered; "yet perhaps we shall see each other once again."

"See each other again?" I answered; "then I am the richer by one belief! and so I shall become richer and richer in belief and in the end all will be but belief for me."

"Dear one!" he cried, "let us be still when words do not help! let us end like men! You are spoiling these last moments for yourself."

Meanwhile, we had come to the harbor.

"One thing more!" he said, when we were beside his ship. "Greet your Diotima! Love each other! be happy, beautiful souls!"

"O my Alabanda," I cried, "why can I not go in your stead?"

"What you are called to is more beautiful," he answered; "hold to it! you belong to her, that fair being is henceforth your world—ah! since there is no happiness without sacrifice, accept me as the sacrifice, O Fate, and leave the lovers in their joy!—"

His heart began to overpower him, and he tore himself from me and leaped into the ship, to shorten the parting for himself and for me. I felt the moment like a thunderclap, on which night and deathly silence followed, but in the midst of this annihilation my soul recovered to hold him back, the dear one who was departing, and my arms sprang out toward him of themselves. "Alas, Alabanda! Alabanda!" I cried, and heard a muffled "Farewell" from the ship.

Hyperion to Bellarmin

As it happened, the vessel that was to take me to Calaurea delayed until late in the day on which Alabanda had gone his way in the morning.

I stayed by the shore and, wearied by the pains of

parting, gazed silently at the sea, hour after hour. My
spirit told over the sorrowful days of my slowly dying
youth and waveringly, like the beautiful dove, flitted over
the time to come. I wanted to strengthen myself, I took
out my long forgotten lute to sing a Song of Fate that
once in happy, heedless youth I had repeated after my
Adamas.

> Ye move up there in the light
>   On easeful ground, blessed Geniuses!
>   Bright divine airs
>   Touch you lightly,
>   As the player's fingers
>   Her holy strings.
>
> Outside of Fate, like the sleeping
>   Babe, the Heavenly Ones breathe;
>   Chastely guarded
>   In modest bud,
>   Ever for them
>   The spirit blooms,
>   And their blessed eyes
>   Gaze in still,
>   Eternal light.
>
> But to us it is given
>   Nowhere to rest,
>   Suffering men
>   Falter and fall
>   Blindly from one
>   Hour to the next,
>   Like water flung down
>   From cliff to cliff,
>   Yearlong into uncertainty.

So I sang to the strings. I had scarcely finished when
a boat arrived; in it I immediately recognized my servant,
who brought me a letter from Diotima.

"So you are still on earth?" she wrote, "and still see
the light of day? I thought I should find you elsewhere,
my love! Sooner than you afterward wished, I received

the letter that you wrote before the battle at Cheshme, and so for a whole week I lived believing that you had thrown yourself into the arms of death, before your servant arrived with the joyful news that you are still alive. Moreover, I had heard only a few days after the battle that the ship on which I knew you to be had blown up with all hands.

"But O sweet voice! again I heard you, once again the speech of the beloved touched me like the air of May, and your beautiful, hopeful joy, the lovely phantom of our future happiness, for a moment deceived me too.

"Dear dreamer, why must I wake you? why can I not say, 'Come, and make them true, the beautiful days that you promised me!' But it is too late, Hyperion, it is too late. Your maiden has withered since you have been gone, a fire in me has slowly consumed me, and there is only a little left. Do not be dismayed! Everything in Nature purifies itself, and everywhere the flower of life frees itself more and more from coarser stuff.

"Dearest Hyperion! little did you think to hear my swan song this year.

Continuation

"Almost as soon as you had gone—nay, even in the days of our parting—it began. A strength in my spirit that made me afraid, an inner life before which the life of earth paled and faltered, like night lights in the red of morning—Shall I say it? I could have wished to go to Delphi and build a temple to the God of Enthusiasm under the cliffs of ancient Parnassus, and, a new Pythia, fire the indolent peoples with divine oracles; and my soul knows that my maidenly mouth would have opened the eyes and unknit the brows of all those godforsaken dullards, so powerful was the spirit of life in me! But my mortal limbs grew wearier and wearier and my tormenting melancholy bore me inexorably down. Ah! often in my quiet arbor I wept over the roses of youth! they faded and faded, and your maiden's cheeks were red only from tears. The trees of old were still there, and the bower of old—there once your Diotima stood, your child, Hyperion, before your happy eyes, a blossom among the blossoms, and the powers of Earth and Heaven met peacefully in her; now she walked a stranger among the buds of May, and her trusted confidants, the lovely plants, nodded to her in friendly wise, but she could only mourn; yet I passed none of them by; yet, one after one, I took leave of all the companions of my youth, the groves and springs and rustling hillocks.

"Ah! as long as I could, I went with sweet effort up to the height where you lived with Notara, and talked of you with our friend, as cheerfully as possible, so that he should not write to you of me; but soon, when her heart grew too loud, the dissembler slipped out into the garden, and now there I was at the railing, above the cliff from which I once looked down with you and out into untrammeled Nature; ah! where once I stood, held by your hands, guarded round by your eyes, in the first trembling warmth of love and would fain have poured my overflowing soul, like sacrificial wine, into the abyss of life, there now I staggered about and bewailed my grief to the wind, and my gaze flitted like a shy bird and scarcely dared to look at the beautiful Earth from which I was to depart.

Continuation

"Thus has it befallen your maiden, Hyperion. Ask not how; seek not to explain this death to yourself! He who thinks to fathom such a fate ends by cursing himself and all things, and yet not a soul is to blame.

"Am I to tell you that grief for you has killed me? oh no! oh no! it was welcome to me, that grief, it gave the death that I carried within me form and grace; 'You die to honor your beloved,' I could tell myself now.—

"Or did my soul grow overripe in all the enchantments

of our love, and is that why, like a restive youth, it will no longer stay in its humble home? speak! was it my heart's exuberance that divorced me from mortal life? did my nature, having known your glorious self, become too proud to be content on this mediocre star? But if you taught it to fly, why do you not also teach my soul to return to you? If you kindled the ether-loving fire, why did you not guard it for me?—Hear me, beloved! for your fair soul's sake, do not accuse yourself of my death!

"Could you hold me back, when your destiny showed you the same road? and if, amid the heroic struggle of your heart, you had preached to me: 'Be satisfied, child! and adapt yourself to the times!' would you not have been the most futile of all the futile?

Continuation

"I will tell you exactly what I believe. Your fire lived in me, your spirit had passed into me; but that could hardly have harmed me, and only your destiny made my new life deadly to me. My soul had grown too strong for me through you, yet through you it would have grown quiet again. You drew my life away from the Earth, but you would also have had power to fetter me to the Earth; you would have conjured my soul into your embracing arms as into a magic circle; ah! a single one of your loving looks would have held me fast, a single one of your loving speeches would have made me a happy, healthy child again; but when a unique destiny bore you away to solitude of spirit as waters are borne to mountain peaks, oh then, when at last I believed that the storm of battle had burst open your prison and my Hyperion had soared up into his old freedom again, only then was all decided for me, and now must soon end.

"I have used many words, yet the great Roman heroine died silent when her Brutus and her country were struggling in the throes of death. What better could I do in the best of my last days of life?—Yet still I feel an urgency to say many things. My life was silent; my death is loquacious. Enough!

Continuation

"I must tell you but one thing more.

"You would have to perish, you would be bound to despair, but the spirit will save you. No laurel will comfort you and no crown of myrtle; Olympus will be your comfort, the living, present Olympus that blooms ever young about all your senses. The beautiful world is my Olympus; in it you will live; and with the holy beings of the world, with the Gods of Nature, with them you will be happy.

"O be ye welcome, ye good and true! ye deeply missed, ye unrecognized! children and eldest of all! Sun and Earth and Ether, with all living souls that play about you, about whom you play, in eternal love! oh, take all-endeavoring mankind, take the fugitives back into the family of the gods, receive them into the home of Nature, from which they fled!—

"You know this word, Hyperion! You began it in me. You will fulfill it in yourself, and then rest.

"I have enough of it to die happily, a Grecian maiden.

"The poor creatures who know nothing but to toil at their trumpery tasks, who serve only necessity and scorn the Genius and pay thee no honor, childlike life of Nature! let them fear death. Their yoke has become their world; they know nothing better than their servitude; they shrink from the divine freedom that death gives us!

"But not I! I have risen above the piecework that human hands have made. I have felt the life of Nature, which is higher than all thought—if I become a plant, would that be so great a loss?—I shall be. How should I be lost from the sphere of life, in which eternal love, common to all, holds all natures together? how should I escape from the union that binds all beings together? It does not break as easily as the loose bonds of this age. It is not like a market day, when the people run together and make a hubbub and part. No! by the spirit that makes us one, by the divine spirit that is each man's own and is common to all! no! no! in the union of Nature fidelity is no dream! We part only to be more intimately one, more divinely at peace with all, with each other. We die that we may live.

"I shall be; I ask not what I shall be. To be, to live— that is enough, that is the honor of the gods; and therefore all things that but have life are equal in the divine world, and in it there are no masters and servants. Natures live together, like lovers; they hold all in common, spirit, joy, and eternal youth.

"The stars have chosen permanence, they float forever in quiet fullness of life and know not age. We represent perfection in mutability; we divide the great harmonies of joy into changing melodies. Like harp players about the thrones of the eldest of all, we live, ourselves divine, among the quiet Gods of the World, with our fleeting lovesong we temper the blissful seriousness of the Sun God and the rest.

"Look up into the world! Is it not like an advancing triumphal procession by which Nature celebrates her eternal victory over all corruption? and does not life lead death with it to glorification, as the general once led captive kings with him? and we, we are the virgins and the youths, who accompany the majestic procession with dance and song in changing shapes and tones.

"Now let me be silent. To say more would be too much. We shall, I must believe, meet again.

"Sorrowing youth! soon, soon will you be happier. Your laurel did not ripen, your myrtles faded, for you shall be the priest of divine Nature, and your days of poetry are already germinating.

"Oh, could I but see you in your future beauty! Farewell."

At the same time I received a letter from Notara, in which he wrote:

"The day after she wrote to you for the last time, she became very quiet, spoke a few words more, and then said that she would rather leave the earth in fire than

be buried, and that we should collect her ashes in an urn
and put them in the forest, in the place where you first
met her. Soon afterward, as it began to grow dark, she
bade us good night, as if she wanted to sleep, and put
her arms around her beautiful head; we heard her breathing until nearly morning. As it became perfectly still then
and I heard nothing more, I went in to her and listened.

"O Hyperion! what else shall I say? It was over, and
our lamenting wakens her no more.

"It is a terrible mystery that such a life must die, and
I will confess to you that I myself have neither mind nor
belief since I saw this happen.

"But a beautiful death is always better, Hyperion! than
such a somnolent life as ours now is.

"To chase away flies is our work in the future; and to
gnaw on the things of the world as children gnaw on the
hard iris-root—that, in the end, is our pleasure. To grow
old among young peoples seems to me a delight, but to
grow old where all is old seems to me worse than anything.—

"I would almost advise you, my Hyperion! not to come
here. I know you. It would drive you out of your mind.
Then too, you are not safe here. My dear friend! think of
Diotima's mother, think of me, and preserve yourself!

"I will confess to you that I shudder when I consider
your fate. But I believe, too, that the burning summer
does not dry up the deep springs, but only the shallow
rain-fed stream. I have seen you at moments, Hyperion,
when you seemed to me a higher being. You are now
put to the test, and it must appear who you are. Farewell."

So Notara wrote; and you ask, my Bellarmin! how it
is with me now, while I tell you of this.

Best of friends! I am at peace, for I want nothing better
than the gods. Must not all things suffer? And the more
excellent, the more deeply! Does not sacred Nature suffer?
O my Divinity! that thou couldst mourn as thou art blissful—that was long beyond my understanding. But the
bliss that does not suffer is sleep, and without death there
is no life. Shouldst thou be eternally like a child, and sleep
like that which is nothing? forego victory? not run through

all perfections? Yes! yes! sorrow is worthy to lie at man's heart and to be thine intimate, O Nature! For it but leads from one bliss to another, and there is no other companion on the way.——

I wrote to Notara, when I began to revive again, from Sicily, to which a ship from Paros first brought me:

"I have obeyed you, my dear Notara! I am already far from my friends in Calaurea and now wish to send you news; but words are hard for me, I must confess. The blessed, among whom Diotima now is, do not speak much; in my night, in the abyss of the mourner, there is an end to speech too.

"My Diotima died a beautiful death; in that you are right; and it is that, too, which awakens me, and gives me back my soul.

"But it is not to the world as it was that I return. I am a stranger, like the unburied when they come up from Acheron, and if I were on my native island, in the gardens of my youth, which my father bars to me, ah! even then, even then I should be a stranger on earth, and no god would join me to the past again.

"Yes! all is over. I must only say that to myself again and again, must bind my soul with it, so that it shall remain quiet and not fire up in senseless, childish efforts.

"All is over; and even if I could weep, beautiful Divinity, as once thou didst weep for Adonis, my Diotima will not come back to me and the word of my heart has lost its power, for only the winds hear me.

"God! that I myself am nothing, and that the meanest workman can say he has done more than I! that they are free to solace themselves, the shallow of mind, and smile and mockingly call me dreamer, because my deeds did not ripen for me, because my arms are not free, because the time in which I live is like the raging Procrustes who, capturing men, put them in a child's cradle and, to make them fit into that little bed, hacked off their limbs!

"If only it were not too utterly desperate to fling myself among the crowd of fools and be torn to pieces! or if only noble blood need not be ashamed to mix with the blood of serfs! oh, if there were a banner, ye Gods! under which my Alabanda might serve, a Thermopylae where

I could honorably let it bleed to death, all the lonely love for which I never find a use! To be sure, it would be better if I could live, could live, and quiet great woe with great joy in the new temples, in the newly assembled Agora of our people; yet I speak not of that, for I but weep my strength wholly away when I think of it all.

"Ah! Notara! it is over with me too; I am weary of my own soul because I reproach it with Diotima's death, and the thoughts of my youth, which I prized so greatly, mean nothing to me now. Did they not poison my Diotima!

"And now tell me, what refuge remains?—Yesterday I went to the summit of Aetna. There I remembered the great Sicilian who, weary of counting the hours, knowing the soul of the World, in his bold joy in life there flung himself down into the glorious flames, for 'the cold poet had to warm himself at the fire,' said someone later, to mock him.

"O how gladly would I have taken such mockery upon myself! but one must think more highly of oneself than I do before, thus unbidden, one can flee to Nature's heart, or whatever else you may be pleased to call it, for, believe me! as I am now I have no names for things and all before me is uncertainty.

"And now, Notara! tell me what refuge remains?

"In Calaurea's woods?—Yes! in the green darkness there where our trees, the faithful witnesses of our love, still stand, where, like the red of evening, their dying foliage falls on Diotima's urn and their beautiful crowns, gradually growing old, bend over Diotima's urn, until they, too, fall upon the beloved ashes—there, there, I could perhaps live as I would!

"But you advise me to stay away, you think that I am not safe in Calaurea, and it may be so.

"I know very well you will tell me to go to Alabanda. But listen! he is destroyed! even that firm, slender tree is mouldering, too, and boys will gather up the chips and make themselves a merry fire with them.

"He has gone; he has certain good friends who will make things easy for him, who are peculiarly skilled in helping out anyone who finds life something of a burden; he has gone to visit them, and why? because there is nothing else for him to do, or, if you would know all, because a passion is eating out his heart, and do you know for whom? for Diotima, whom he believes to be still alive and married to me and happy—poor Alabanda! now she belongs to us both!

"He traveled into the east, and I am taking a ship northwestward, because chance will have it so.—

"And now a farewell to all of you! all you dear ones who have been close to my heart, friends of my youth and you my parents, and all you dear Greeks, you sufferers!

"Ye airs that nourished me in tender childhood, and ye dark laurel woods and ye cliffs by the shore and ye majestic waters that taught my soul to surmise your greatness—and ah! ye monuments of sorrow, where my melancholy began, ye sacred walls with which the heroic cities girdle themselves, and ye ancient gates through which many a beautiful traveler passed, ye temple pillars and thou rubble of the gods! and thou, O Diotima! and ye valleys of my love, and ye brooks that once saw her blessed form, ye trees where she rejoiced, ye springtimes in which she lived, lovely with her flowers, depart not, depart not from me! yet if it must be, ye sweet memories! grow dim ye too and leave me, for man can change nothing and the light of life comes and departs as it will."

Hyperion to Bellarmin

So I arrived among the Germans. I did not demand much and was prepared to find even less. I came there humbly, like homeless, blind Oedipus to the gates of Athens, where the sacred grove received him; and fair souls came to greet him—

How different my experience!

Barbarians from the remotest past, whom industry and science and even religion have made yet more barbarous, profoundly incapable of any divine emotion, disqualified to the marrow for the delights of the sacred Graces, of-

fensive to every well-conditioned soul through the whole
gamut from pretense to pettiness, hollow and tuneless,
like the shards of a discarded pot—such, my Bellarmin!
were my comforters.

It is a hard saying, and yet I speak it because it is
the truth: I can think of no people more at odds with
themselves than the Germans. You see artisans, but no
men, thinkers, but no men, priests, but no men, masters
and servants, but no men, minors and adults, but no men
—is this not like a battlefield on which hacked-off hands
and arms and every other member lie pell-mell, while the
life-blood flows from them to vanish in the sand?

Everyone follows his own trade, you will tell me, and
I say the same. Only, he must follow it with his whole
soul, must not stifle every power in him that does not
precisely accord with his official designation, must not,
with this niggardly anxiety, literally and hypocritically be
only what he is called; let him be what he is, earnestly,
lovingly, then a spirit lives in all that he does; and if he
is forced into an occupation in which the spirit may not
live, let him cast it off with scorn and learn to plow! But
your Germans choose not to go beyond the barest necessities, which is the reason why there is so much botched
work among them and so little that is free, that gives any
genuine pleasure. Yet that could be overlooked, were not
such men of necessity insensitive to all comely living, did
not the curse of godforsaken unnature everywhere lie upon such a people.—

"The virtues of the Ancients were but glittering vices,"
was once said by some malicious tongue (I forget whose);
and yet their vices themselves are virtues, for a childlike,
beautiful spirit still lived in them, and of all that they did
nothing was done without soul. But the virtues of the
Germans are glittering vices and nothing more; for they
are but forced labor, wrung from the sterile heart in craven
fear, with the toil of slaves, and they impart no comfort
to any pure soul that fain would draw its sustenance from
Beauty, that, ah! made fastidious by the sacred harmony
in noble natures, cannot bear the discord that cries out in
all the dead order of these men.

I tell you: there is nothing sacred that is not desecrated,

is not debased to a miserable expedient among this people; and what even among savages is usually preserved in sacred purity, these all-calculating barbarians pursue as one pursues any trade, and cannot do otherwise; for where a human being is once conditioned to look, there it serves its ends, seeks its profit, it dreams no more—God forbid!—it remains sedate; and when it makes holiday and when it loves and when it prays, and even when spring's lovely festival, when the season of reconciliation for the world dissolves all cares and conjures innocence into a guilty heart, when, intoxicated by the sun's warm rays, the slave in his joy forgets his chains, and the enemies of mankind, softened by the divinely living air, are as peaceable as children—when the caterpillar itself grows wings and the bees swarm, even then the German sticks to his last and scarcely deigns to notice the weather!

But thou wilt sit in judgment, sacred Nature! For were they but modest, these people, did they but not make themselves a law unto the better among them! did they but revile not what they are not, yet even that could be condoned in them, did they but not mock the divine!—

Or is not that divine which you Germans mock and call soulless? Is not the air that you drink in better than your chatter? are not the sun's rays nobler than all of you in your cleverness? the earth's springs and the morning dew refresh your forests; can you too do as much? ah! you can kill, but you cannot bring to life, unless it is done by love, which proceeds not from you, which you did not invent. You worry and contrive, that you may escape Fate, and cannot understand it when your childish arts are unavailing; and meanwhile the stars move innocently on above you. Where she tolerates you, you degrade and mangle patient Nature, yet she lives on, in eternal youth, and you cannot drive away her autumn and her spring, you corrupt not her ether.

Oh, she must indeed be divine, since you are permitted to destroy and she grows not old and despite you Beauty remains beautiful!—

It is heart-rending, too, to see your poets, your artists, and all those who still honor the Genius, who love and cultivate Beauty. The poor good creatures live in the world like strangers in their own house, they are exactly like long-suffering Ulysses when he sat at his door disguised as a beggar while the shameless suitors rioted in the hall and asked, "Who sent us this vagabond?"

Their Muse-inspired youths grow up for the German people full of love and spirit and hope; see them seven years later, and they are wandering about like shades, silent and cold, they are like a soil that the enemy has sown with salt so that it shall never put forth a blade of grass, and when they speak, alas for him who understands them! for him who in their raging Titan strength, as in their protean arts, can see the desperate battle that their beautiful, troubled spirit wages against the barbarians with whom it is forced to deal!

"Everything on earth is imperfect," is the Germans' old refrain. If only someone would once tell these people whom God has forsaken that everything is so imperfect among them only because they leave nothing pure uncorrupted, nothing sacred untouched by their coarse hands, that nothing thrives among them because they do not respect the root of all thriving, divine Nature, that life with them is stale and burdened with cares and too-too full of cold, silent discord, because they scorn the Genius, which brings power and nobility into human endeavor, and serenity into suffering, and love and brotherhood to towns and houses.

And that too is why they are so afraid of death and, for the sake of their molluscan existence, bear every indignity, for they know nothing higher than the bungling job that they have made of things.

O Bellarmin, where a people loves Beauty, where it honors the Genius in its own artists, there a common spirit is astir like the breath of life, there the shy mind opens, self-conceit melts away, and all hearts are reverent and great and enthusiasm brings forth heroes. The home of all men is with such a people and gladly can the stranger linger there. But where divine Nature and her artists are so insulted, ah! there life's greatest joy is gone, and any other star is better than earth. There men grow ever more sterile, ever more empty, who yet were all born beautiful; servility increases and with its insolence, intoxication grows

with troubles and, with luxury, hunger and dread of star-
vation; the blessing of each year becomes a curse, and all
gods flee.

And alas for the stranger who journeys in love and
comes to such a people, and alas and alas and alas again
for him who comes to such a people as I came, driven
by great grief, a beggar as I was a beggar!—

Enough! you know me, and will take this in good part,
Bellarmin! I spoke in your name too, I spoke for all who
are in that country and who suffer as I suffered there.

Hyperion to Bellarmin

I now wanted to leave Germany. I looked for nothing
more among these people, I had been sufficiently offended
by relentless affronts, I was unwilling to let my soul bleed
to death among such men.

But the heavenly spring detained me; it was the only
pleasure that remained to me, it was indeed my last love,
how could I think of other things and leave the country
where spring too was?

Bellarmin! never had I so fully experienced the old un-
changing decree of Fate that a new bliss rises in the heart
when it perseveres and suffers through the midnight of
anguish, and that, like nightingale voices in the dark, the
world's song of life first sounds divinely for us in deep
affliction. For I now lived with the blooming trees as with
geniuses; and the clear brooks that flowed under them
whispered the care from my breast like divine voices. And
so it befell me everywhere, dear friend!—when I lay in
the grass and tender life grew green around me; when I
climbed the warm hill on which the rose grew wild about
the stone path; and when I rowed along the gay river
shore and among all the islands that the river tenderly
protects.

And when on many a morning, as the sick to medicinal
springs, I climbed to the mountain's summit through the
sleeping flowers, but all about me, sated with sweet sleep,

the dear birds flew out of the foliage, reeling in the half-light and craving the day, and the more active air now carried up the prayers of the valleys, the voices of the flocks, and the notes of the morning bells, and now the high light, divinely serene, followed its accustomed path, enchanting the Earth with immortal life, so that her heart grew warm and all her children felt their existence again —oh! like the moon, which still waited in the sky to share the joy of day, I stood lonely too above the plains and wept loving tears down to the shores and the shining waters and for a long time could not turn away my eyes.

Or at evening, when I wandered far into the valley, to the cradle of the spring, where the dark oak tops rustled around me and Nature buried me in her peace like one who dies a blessed death; when the earth was a shadow, and invisible life whispered among the branches, among the summits; and over the summits hung the still evening cloud, a shining mountain from which heaven's rays flowed down to me, like brooks to quench the traveler's thirst—

"O Sun, O ye breezes," I cried, "by ye alone my heart still lives, as among brothers!"

Thus more and more I surrendered myself to blessed Nature, and almost too endlessly. How gladly would I have become a child again to be nearer to her, how gladly would I have known less and become like the pure ray of light to be nearer to her! oh, one moment in her peace, to feel her beauty, oh, how much more it meant to me than years full of thought, than all the endeavors of all-endeavoring mankind! What I had learned, what I had done in my life, dissolved like ice, and all the projects of youth died away in me; O ye loved ones far away, ye dead and ye living, how intimately at one we were!

Once I sat far in the fields, by a spring, in the shadow of ivy-green cliffs and overhanging shrubs in flower. It was the fairest noonday I have known. Sweet breezes blew and the land still shone in morning freshness and the light smiled silently from its native ether. The laborers had all gone home to eat and rest from their work; my love was alone with the springtime and in me was an inconceivable longing. "Diotima," I cried, "where are you, oh, where are you?" And it seemed to me that I heard

Diotima's voice, the voice that cheered me in the days of happiness—

"I am with my kindred," she cried, "with your kindred, whom the erring minds of men know not."

A gentle terror seized me and my thought fell asleep.

"O dear word from holy mouth," I cried when again I awakened, "dear riddle, do I understand you?"

And once more I looked back into the cold night of men, and shuddered and wept for joy that I was so blessed; and I uttered words, I think, but they were like the roar of fire when it flies up and leaves the ashes behind—

"O thou," so I thought, "with thy gods, Nature! I have dreamed it out, the dream of human things, and I say, Only thou livest, and what they who know no peace have attempted and conceived melts away from thy flame like beads of wax!

"How long have they gone without thee? oh, how long have their tribe abused thee, called thee and thy gods common, thy living gods, thy silent, blissful gods!

"Men fall from thee like rotten fruits, oh, let them perish, for thus they return to thy root; so may I, too, O tree of life, that I may grow green again with thee and breathe thy crown about me with all thy budding twigs! peacefully and devoutly, for we are all sprung from the same golden seed!

"Ye springs of earth! ye flowers! and ye woods and ye eagles and thou, brotherly light! how old and new is our love!—We are free, we are not narrowly alike in outward semblance; how should the mode of Life not vary? yet we love the ether, all of us, and in the inmost of our inmost selves we are alike.

"We too, we too are not parted, Diotima, and tears for you understand it not. Living tones are we, we sound together in thy harmony, Nature! which who can undo? who can part lovers?—

"O Soul! Soul! Beauty of the World! indestructible, ravishing one! with thine eternal youth! thou art; what, then, is death and all the woe of men?—Ah! those strange creatures have spoken many empty words. Yet from delight all comes, and all ends in peace.

"Like lovers' quarrels are the dissonances of the world. Reconciliation is there, even in the midst of strife, and all things that are parted find one another again.

"The arteries separate and return to the heart and all is one eternal glowing life."

So I thought. More soon.

Author's Preface to Volume I*

I should be glad if I could promise this book the affection of the German people. But I fear that some of them will read it as a treatise and be too greatly concerned with the *fabula docet,* whereas others will take it too lightly, and that neither the former nor the latter will understand it.

He who merely inhales the scent of my plant does not know it, and he who plucks it merely in order to learn from it does not know it either.

The resolution of dissonances in a particular character is neither for mere reflection nor for empty pleasure.

The scene of the events which follow is not new, and I confess that I was once childish enough to try to alter the book in this respect, but I soon became convinced that it was the only scene appropriate to Hyperion's elegiac character and was ashamed that the presumable verdict of the public had rendered me so excessively pliable.

I regret that for the present it is not possible for everyone to judge of the plan of the book. But the second volume will follow as soon as possible.

*Prefixed to Volume I, which contained only Part One, published in 1797. Volume II (Part Two) did not follow until 1799.—Tr.

Translator's Afterword

That a work by one of the world's great poets, to which he devoted years of his creative life, should, more than a century and a half after its publication, still be unavailable in English is reason enough for attempting a translation of it.

Genius apart—and, no less than the work of a genius, it is a work of genius—*Hyperion* is essentially a fiction of the Romantic Age, of the same genre as Byron's *Corsair* (Alabanda, too, was a corsair) or Shelley's *Zastrozzi*. Shelley, born in the same year that *Hyperion* was first conceived (1792), with the *Zastrozzi* and *St. Irvyne* of his youth and the *Coliseum* and the "Scenes from Goethe's *Faust*" of his early maturity, would have been its ideal translator.

A hundred and fifty years later, what would have been natural for him creates difficulties. At least since T. S. Eliot decreed the bastardy of the prose poem, we are no longer accustomed to prose at such a high pitch. If that most mechanical of indications, the exclamation point, is not enough, the basic level of discourse is succinctly apparent in the fact that almost no one in *Hyperion* ever *says* anything, it is always "he cried" (the equivalent in Shelley being "exclaimed he"). Nor are we accustomed to rhetoric at such a high pitch. To be sure, Faulkner has done something to subvert the Hemingway canon of the short simple declarative sentence. But Faulkner's long sentences, even when they continue for several paragraphs, tend to be agglutinative. Hölderlin's long sentences, which also sometimes continue for several paragraphs, are logical structures firmly in the rhetorical tradition that runs from Isocrates through Quintilian and Martianus Capella to the Renaissance Humanists and, in English, to Walter Savage Landor.

I will only say that, faced with these problems, I very soon became convinced that valor was the better part of discretion. Deliberately ignoring contemporary literary practice, I have neither toned down the fervor of *Hyperion* nor trimmed down its rhetoric. Written as ecstatic Romantic fiction, it can exist, though in another language and another age, only as ecstatic Romantic fiction. To try to make it anything else would be to make it nothing.

W. R. T.

SIGNET CLASSICS
from Around the World

THE CONFESSIONS OF FELIX KRULL *by Thomas Mann*
This novel of high comedy and brilliant parody retraces the career of an extraordinary swindler *par excellence*. Translated by Denver Lindley. Afterword by George Steiner.
(#CT188—75¢)

THE MARK OF THE BEAST and Other Stories
by Rudyard Kipling
Fifteen of the finest of Kipling's timeless, vividly realistic tales, set in India, England, America, and Europe. Foreword by Roger Burlingame. (#CD246—50¢)

THE TRAVELS OF MARCO POLO
The enduring record of Marco Polo's thirty-five years of fabulous Eastern travel. Edited with an Introduction by Milton Rugoff. (#CD97—50¢)

CANDIDE, ZADIG and Selected Stories *by Voltaire*
Voltaire satirizes with ruthless wit the social, religious, and human vanities of his day in sixteen biting stories. A new translation with an Introduction by Donald Frame.
(#CD35—50¢)

THE MARQUISE OF O—and Other Stories
by Heinrich von Kleist
The title story and seven other tales, revealing the bold quality of von Kleist's art. Translated by Martin Greenberg. Foreword by Thomas Mann. (#CT126—75¢)

RESURRECTION *by Leo Tolstoy*
The Russian master's final work tells the story of a young man who seeks salvation by following into exile the girl for whose career in crime he was responsible. Translated by Vera Traill with a Foreword by Alan Hodge.
(#CT63—75¢)

OLIVER TWIST *by Charles Dickens*
Dickens' classic indictment of the orphanages and crime-ridden slums of 19th Century London. Afterword by Edward Le Comte. (#CP102—60¢)

THE SCARLET LETTER *by Nathaniel Hawthorne*
A masterpiece by one of America's fine 19th Century writers, this is the story of a proud and sinful woman in Puritan New England. Foreword by Leo Marx. (#CD8—50¢)

THE RIDER ON THE WHITE HORSE and Selected Stories
  by Theodor Storm

A unique selection of eight *novellen by* the 19th century German master of this literary genre. New translation with Foreword by James Wright. (#CT262—75¢)

THE DIARY OF A MADMAN and Other Stories *by Nikolai Gogol*

New translation by Andrew MacAndrew of the title story and *The Nose, The Carriage, The Overcoat,* and the historical romance, *Taras Bulba.* Afterword by Leon Stilman.
(#CP285—60¢)

MANON LESCAUT *by Abbé Prevost*

The first modern "novel of passion" on which the operas of Massenet and Puccini are based. Newly translated with an Introduction by Donald Frame. (#CP96—60¢)

THE PRINCESS OF CLEVES *by Mme. de Lafayette*

A profound and delicate psychological novel about a woman involved in a triangle. Newly translated with a Foreword by Walter J. Cobb. (#CD89—50¢)

GULLIVER'S TRAVELS *by Jonathan Swift*

The four classic voyages of Gulliver, which make both a fascinating fairy tale and a bitter satire. With 30 illustrations by Charles Brock and 5 maps. Foreword by Marcus Cunliffe.
(#CD14—50¢)

HEART OF DARKNESS AND THE SECRET SHARER
  by Joseph Conrad

Two tragic stories—one of a tragedy at sea, the other of a man's deterioration in an isolated trading post in the ivory country—by one of the world's great writers. Introduction by Albert J. Guerard. (#CD4—50¢)

THE SORROWS OF YOUNG WERTHER and Selected Writings
  by Johann Wolfgang von Goethe

The title story, two tales, and excerpts from Goethe's autobiography. New translation by Catherine Hutter. Foreword by Hermann J. Weigand. (#CP140—60¢)

BILLY BUDD and Other Tales *by Herman Melville*

The title story and other outstanding short stories, including the *Piazza Tales,* by the author of *Moby Dick.* Afterword by Willard Thorp. (#CT75—75¢)

ARROWSMITH *by Sinclair Lewis*

The moving story of an idealistic American physician who struggles against the materialists who seek to dominate his life. Afterword by Mark Schorer. (#CT92—75¢)

ROBINSON CRUSOE *by Daniel Defoe*

The timeless story of a young merchant seaman's struggle for survival when he is marooned on an uninhabited island. Afterword by Harvey Swados. (#CD55—50¢)

THE MARRIAGES and Other Stories *by Henry James*

Nine rarely anthologized stories by the master of sophisticated irony. Foreword by Eleanor M. Tilton.

(#CD87—50¢)

YOUNG TORLESS *by Robert Musil*

A military boarding school is the setting for this penetrating novel about the intellectual and sexual awakening of a highly sensitive young boy. Translated by Ernst Kaiser and Eithne Wilkins. Afterword by John Simon. (#CT266—75¢)

MAIN STREET *by Sinclair Lewis*

The crusade of a doctor's wife against the narrow-minded conventions of a small town. Afterword by Mark Schorer.

(#CT93—75¢)

BABBITT *by Sinclair Lewis*

The caustic portrayal of an American go-getter, ready and willing to sacrifice his principles to get ahead. Afterword by Mark Schorer. (#CT91—75¢)

THE MUTINY ON BOARD H.M.S. BOUNTY *by William Bligh*

The captain's own account of the most famous mutiny to take place in the South Seas. Afterword by Milton Rugoff.

(#CP94—60¢)

TO OUR READERS: If your dealer does not have the SIGNET and MENTOR books you want, you may order them by mail enclosing the list price plus 10c a copy to cover mailing. If you would like our free catalog, please request it by postcard. The New American Library, Inc., P. O. Box 2310, Grand Central Station, New York, N. Y., 10017.